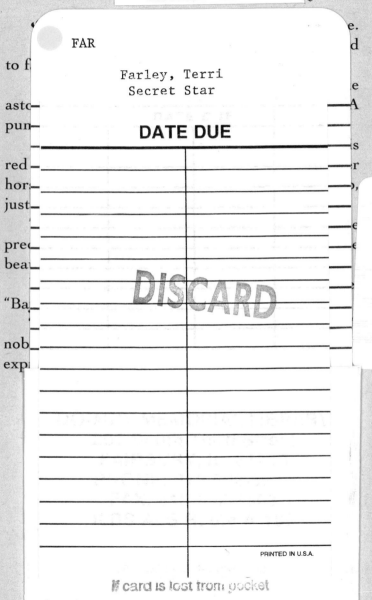

FAR

Farley, Terri
Secret Star

DATE DUE

DISCARD

PRINTED IN U.S.A.

If card is lost from pocket

e.
d

to f

e

asto A

pun s

red r

hor),

just

e

pre e

bea

"Ba

nob

exp

Read all the books about the

Phantom Stallion

1

THE WILD ONE

2

MUSTANG MOON

3

DARK SUNSHINE

4

THE RENEGADE

5

FREE AGAIN

6

THE CHALLENGER

7

DESERT DANCER

8

GOLDEN GHOST

Phantom Stallion

⋐ 19 ⋑
Secret Star

TERRI FARLEY

AVON BOOKS

An Imprint of HarperCollins*Publishers*

Library of Congress Catalog Card Number: 2005901989

ISBN-10: 0-06-075847-3 — ISBN-13: 978-0-06-075847-9

First Avon edition, 2006

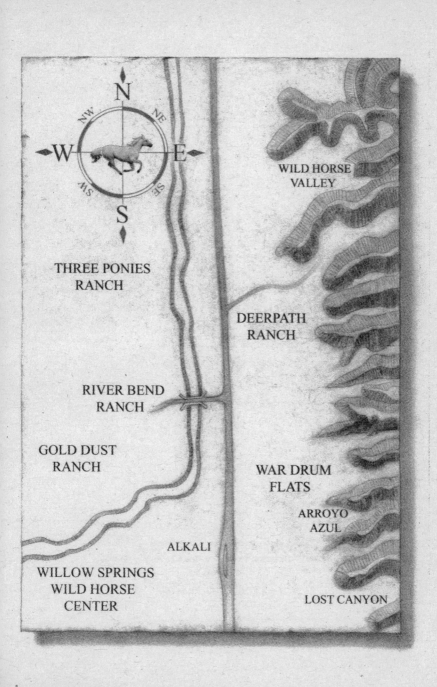

Chapter One ∞

Tempest had discovered her own neigh, and she wasn't afraid to use it.

Sam tried to escape the blast of high-pitched sound by pressing her spine against the wooden boards of the box stall and her palms against her ears. It didn't help much, but finally, the black filly stopped to draw a breath.

"Enough, baby," Sam crooned. "All the other horses can hear you. They know you're the princess of River Bend Ranch."

Sam wished she could make Tempest understand, because any minute a movie star horse and his trainer would be driving over the bridge to River Bend Ranch. For a few days, Tempest wouldn't be the center of attention, even though the filly really was River Bend's princess. Tempest's sire was the swift and powerful silver stallion known as the Phantom. No one could deny he was a king among wild horses.

Tempest's mother, Dark Sunshine, had roamed free as the Phantom's queen until she'd reluctantly chosen the ranch as the safest place for her filly.

Sassy and proud, Tempest seemed totally aware of her heritage, and with two celebrities on the ranch, the filly might not get all the attention she thought she deserved.

Now, even Dark Sunshine had had enough of Tempest's shrill neighs.

"Hey Sunny, you're not leaving me here alone with her, are you?" Sam called after the buckskin mare.

Dark Sunshine didn't glance back. Shaking her black mane so hard that half of it flipped from the right side of her neck to the left, the mustang mare slipped out of the box stall into the corral.

Sam told herself she only imagined Sunny's sigh at the peace and quiet of the grassy enclosure.

Hands on her hips, Sam surveyed her morning's work. She'd cleaned all the stalls in the barn, raking out the soiled bedding and replacing it with sweet-smelling straw. She'd paid special attention to the big box stall where the star stallion would stay when he wasn't in the corral adjoining the one Tempest shared with her mother.

Inez Garcia and Bayfire. Excitement sprinkled

down on Sam like bright confetti. Having two Hollywood celebrities right here on the ranch was almost unreal. She could hardly believe Maxine Ely, her friend Jake's mom, actually knew Inez Garcia and had recommended she and her stunt stallion stay at River Bend Ranch for a few days before shooting a scene in Lost Canyon.

Just two nights ago, Inez Garcia had called after talking with Jake's mom. Sam wished she'd been the one to answer the phone, but Brynna had left the dinner table just as the phone rang, so she'd been the lucky one.

"The rest of the crew is staying in Alkali," Brynna had said, after she'd explained the other details. Then she'd looked at Sam and added, pointedly, "But Inez would like Bayfire's time here to be private."

Sam knew she'd sucked in a loud, disappointed breath before she blurted, "Does that mean I can't tell anyone?"

There hadn't been a minute for negotiation.

"That's right," Brynna had said. "Not even Jen."

"Where on earth will we put a movie star?" Gram had said. She'd bolted to her feet and begun gathering dishes and clearing the table as if she needed to start preparing that instant.

"She'll stay in her camper," Brynna had said. "And she made it very clear, she's just a horse trainer. In fact, her only concern is for her horse. She obviously loves him."

At that, Dad had laughed. "Who wouldn't? If I owned the highest paid stunt horse in America, I'd love him, too."

"Oh Wyatt," Brynna had said, making a gesture to brush aside Dad's cynicism.

Now, as fresh straw rustled under Tempest's hooves, Sam wondered if Dad was right.

"Well, I love you, whether you can do anything or not," Sam told Tempest.

She bent, grabbed a handful of straw, and waved it to amuse the filly.

With a side swipe of her black muzzle, Tempest knocked the straw from Sam's hand. Then she stamped a front hoof, lifted her chin, and tried to stare over Sam's head.

"Don't talk back to me, young lady," Sam said, trying not to laugh at the filly's pose.

Maybe Tempest was bored with Sam's lecturing. Maybe she'd snuffled up dust that hadn't settled from Sam's raking. Whatever the reason, the filly began snorting and rolling her eyes.

As if he thought the foal's shrill neighs were about to start up again, Blaze, the ranch Border collie, gave a quick yap and bounded out of the barn.

In response, the filly gave a teeter-totter kick toward the barn's rafters. When Sam didn't scurry away too, Tempest's ears pricked forward and her brown eyes turned studious.

Sam tightened her stubby ponytail. Then, arms

hanging loose from the short sleeves of her faded pink T-shirt, legs relaxed in her jeans and boots, she tilted her head to one side.

Loosen up and settle down, her body language told the filly, and as she watched Tempest watch her, Sam fought back a yawn.

Tempest wasn't the only noisy one today.

The morning sky had been more black than blue when Sam had first looked out her bedroom window to see why a blue jay wouldn't stop squawking.

Finally she'd spotted a winged shadow dive-bombing Cougar, her tiger-striped cat, as he tried to slink across the ranch yard.

Cougar must have slipped outside at Dad's heels without him noticing, because the cat wasn't allowed outside the house during the hours coyotes might be around. But the ranch was a compact little world of its own, and nothing stayed secret for long.

"You're caught," Sam had said through the window-pane, though there was no way the cat could hear her.

As the cat and bird had moved farther from the two-story white ranch house, Sam had climbed back into bed, hoping for a few more minutes of sleep.

It hadn't worked. Just seconds later Brynna's hair dryer began howling from the bathroom down the hall.

Even though it was Saturday, her stepmother and Gram had risen early, rushing to do some errands in

Darton before Inez Garcia and Bayfire arrived.

Sam had pulled the pillow over her head, trying to drown out the sound, but then the vacuum cleaner had started droning downstairs.

Though Inez Garcia had insisted she didn't want any special treatment, Sam wasn't surprised by Gram's last-minute housekeeping.

Gram had probably baked something delicious, too, but if so, she'd hidden it. When Sam made her way down into the kitchen for breakfast, Gram and Brynna were gone and she'd been left with nothing but cold cereal and toast.

Tired of Sam's daydreaming, Tempest gave a low nicker.

"Save your voice." Sam coaxed the filly. "I've had enough noise this morning."

As if Sam had thrown down a dare, Tempest extended her tiny muzzle upward and released another ear-splitting whinny.

Over the foal's racket, Sam heard hammering and a rumble outside the barn. Dad was starting up his new tractor.

Sam sighed. She guessed she should go out and admire the machine, even though she didn't understand Dad's decision to buy it.

By entering a drawing at the rodeo, she'd won Dad a brand-new truck equipped with every luxury imaginable. Besides its off-road ability, the truck had a windshield tinted to cut the glare of the desert sun, heated seats to warm predawn trips out to break the ice off the cattle's water, and a sound system that surrounded you with music real enough that you might have been onstage with the band.

But Sam only knew this from the brochure that had come with the winner's certificate. Dad had turned down the truck.

Instead of starting it up and shouting "yippee" all the way home, he'd made an agreement with the dealer. Dad had traded in his old tractor. Its value, added to the price of the prize truck, had equaled the cost of a six-year-old steel-gray truck, which was nice enough, and a state-of-the-art tractor that did everything, he said, except plant the hay and sell it to the highest bidder.

"I'm out of here," Sam told the filly.

Tempest stopped neighing and followed so close that Sam felt the warmth of the filly's body. Then Tempest wiggled her head between Sam's side and arm, forcing a hug.

Smiling, Sam turned to face her.

Looking up from under long eyelashes, the filly gazed into Sam's face.

"Could you be any cuter?" Sam asked.

The tension in Sam's shoulders and the ringing in her ears vanished.

She'd never believed she could love another horse as much as she did Ace and the Phantom, but her heart had room for one more.

Sam hugged Tempest's neck, then lowered her lips to the filly's cupped black ear and whispered, "Xanadu."

The name was their secret. Sam never stopped imagining where the mythical place called Xanadu might be. Was it the secret valley where the Phantom kept his herd, an invisible place that hovered here between them, or someplace she and the filly had yet to discover together?

"That's what I hope," Sam said.

Once she'd wrung all the attention she needed from Sam, Tempest gave another high-pitched whinny and trotted off to the barn corral to annoy her mother.

Dad had said she could take Ace out for a ride as soon as she'd completed her chores and welcomed Inez Garcia. Sam wondered how long that would take.

A deeper neigh summoned Sam to the ten-acre pasture.

Ace. How did he know she'd been thinking about their ride?

Sam took a deep breath. She was excited about meeting Bayfire, but greeting a stranger, especially one from Hollywood, made her feel kind of shy.

Still, it was better than running around Darton with Gram and Brynna and lots better than haying with Dad and the hands.

Rushing toward the tack room, Sam almost collided with Pepper.

The red-haired cowboy, River Bend's youngest, dodged aside, but his eyes were on Tempest, not Sam.

"She's a beauty," Pepper said, nodding toward the filly at the same time he edged open the door to Blackbeard's Closet. When no avalanche of supplies covered his boots, he added, "I bet you'll be glad when she's grown up, so you'll have a good-lookin' horse to ride."

Sam rarely pictured herself astride a grown-up Tempest. Blue-black and high-stepping, she would be amazing, but that was a long time away.

"I guess," Sam said, "but I have Ace."

"Your Ace isn't much for flashy," Pepper said as he refilled his nail pouch from a box on an over-crowded shelf.

Are you insulting my horse? Sam barely kept her words behind closed lips. It would have been easy to snap at Pepper, but he probably didn't intend to be mean about Ace.

"Better get what I came for," Sam said.

She took a quick look around the tack room for mice and the snakes that considered them tasty snacks.

"Nobody here," Sam muttered.

By the time she'd taken her saddle, blanket, and bridle from their hooks, she still hadn't shaken off Pepper's comment about Ace.

Since Ace couldn't speak up for himself, Sam decided she had no choice but to do it for him.

"Aren't you the one who told me there's no bad color for a horse?" she began, just as Pepper was about to leave the barn.

Pepper didn't pretend not to know what she was talking about.

"Well, yeah, but we're not talkin' just color. You've gotta admit Ace is runty lookin'," Pepper said, grinning.

Sam wouldn't let herself be joshed out of defending her mustang.

"Ace is a great horse and—" she insisted.

"Never said he wasn't," Pepper told her. "To my way of thinkin' he's one of the best horses on this ranch. I'm just sayin'—"

"*I'm* just saying I appreciate him for more than his looks!"

"Have it your way," Pepper said. Then he gave a smile of surrender. "Guess if it weren't for girls like you, guys like me and Ace wouldn't have much to live for."

As Pepper walked off chuckling, Sam tightened her hold on her gear and picked her way around Blaze. The Border collie fanned his tail at half-mast and watched Sam's face.

"Don't ask me what he's talking about," Sam mumbled, and the dog trotted off across the yard on some errand of his own.

Then she hurried, hoping she could get Ace saddled and tied, ready for a quick getaway after the Hollywood boarders arrived.

Sam was rushing so fast, she didn't realize Dad had turned off the tractor. As he stepped around the vehicle, into her path, Dad grinned with pride.

"What do you think?" he asked, jerking a thumb toward the tractor.

In fact, she thought it was a pretty boring machine, but Dad misinterpreted her slow answer.

"Hope I didn't hurt your feelings by tradin'—" he began.

Sam shook her head, then hefted her saddle closer.

"It's not that," she said, wondering if she was likely to get more chores if she told the truth. She did, anyway. "The truck seemed more fun. And the old tractor was still working." She gave a shrug.

"This one's a lot more fuel efficient," Dad said. "It doesn't pollute as much."

Sam imagined the saddle growing heavier as Dad droned on.

". . . thinking about next year, when I won't have as much help around here . . ."

Suddenly, Sam really listened.

Why would Dad be short of help next year?

Everyone on River Bend Ranch did their part. Gram kept the ranch accounts, cooked, and gardened, and was Dad's partner in the business of ranching. Brynna and Sam shared horse responsibilities with Jake Ely.

Jake was one of Sam's two best friends, and even

though he wasn't a member of the family, Dad treated him like one, paying him what he could when he could.

Before Sam could put her worries into words, a door squeaked. Blaze wiggled out from the shade under the wooden porch as a silver-haired figure emerged from the bunkhouse.

Dallas was the ranch foreman. He worked with Dad, overseeing everything to do with cattle and the upkeep of the ranch, and that included assigning Pepper and Ross their cowboying duties each day.

Dallas suffered from arthritis, but she couldn't imagine the ranch without him. She'd never heard him mention family elsewhere, so surely he wasn't leaving.

Sam took a deep breath. Everyone, including the horses and Blaze, had work to do.

"Sam?" Dad said, trying to catch her attention once more.

Sam barely heard him. She glanced at Pepper and Ross, still hammering away.

. . . next year, when I won't have as much help . . .

"Why won't you have as much help?" Sam asked.

"Oh, that's what's got you spooked." Dad placed a hand on her shoulder and his voice turned smooth, as if he were talking to a jumpy horse. "It's nothin' you don't already know. We can't count on Jake being here, of course." Dad said. "I'm ninety-nine percent sure he'll be gone away."

Chapter Two ☙

"Oh, right," Sam said.

Her stomach felt queasy, but she didn't ask why Jake wouldn't be here.

She knew.

In two weeks, Sam would begin her sophomore year at Darton High School, but Jake would start his senior year. His last year of high school. After that, he'd go to college.

Why did her heart dive at that thought? Even though Jake was a buckaroo, he'd been saving money to pay college tuition as long as she could remember.

She was pretty sure the closest university was five hours away. Jake would have to live there, in a student dormitory. That's why Dad couldn't count on Jake to help around the ranch after this year.

"Are you saying you got the new tractor to replace Jake?" Sam asked. It was a weak joke, but Dad answered with an understanding smile.

Too understanding, Sam thought. She straightened and hefted the saddle higher.

The last thing she wanted was to get all sentimental over Jake.

In fact, she refused to do that. The only reason she was feeling emotional was because of that stupid remark Pepper had made about Ace.

And there he was. The bay gelding stood with his head over the gate, waiting for her.

"Hey, good boy," she called to Ace.

He wasn't that tall, but so what? Neither was she. Fourteen hands was just the right size for her. And Ace was the perfect partner. Every inch of him was fast and tough, hardened by generations of horses who'd lived on the open range.

And Ace was smart. His ancestors hadn't been coddled in barns or buckled up in cozy blankets. They'd had to outwit predators, and find food and shelter for themselves.

Ace pawed impatiently, so she answered him.

"Soon as I get you tacked up, and we greet our Hollywood guests, we're out of here."

Ace must have thought she'd said they were leaving now, because he plunged his open mouth toward the bit.

"You're too helpful," Sam told the gelding as she fumbled to get the headstall in place behind his ears.

"Drives me crazy not getting out there earlier," Dad was saying to Dallas as Sam led Ace across the ranch yard to the hitching rail. "But dew-wet hay just clogs things up. Then time's wasted *un*clogging."

"Guess the sun's high enough now that it's dried some," Dallas said, agreeing with Dad. Then he focused his sharp eyes on Sam. "And you're stayin' around to meet this Hollywood horse trainer?"

"Yeah." Sam tried to sound long-suffering, but she could tell she wasn't fooling Dad. He knew she was excited. Still, she added, "Somebody's got to, I guess."

"Sure couldn't get me to do it," Dallas said. "I prefer to spend my time with folks who do real work for a livin'."

Dallas squinted Sam's way, as if he expected her to defend Inez Garcia and her type.

Why was she so excited about their visitors, when everyone else was matter-of-fact? Before Sam answered her own question, Dallas went on.

"Seems to me that askin' a horse to prove his grit by jumpin' off a cliff don't make sense. Fact is, any horse that'd do that without a fire lickin' at his tail needs a lesson in stayin' alive."

"Do they really want him to jump off a cliff?" Sam asked. She hadn't heard about that.

"Somethin' like that," Dad said. "I guess he used to do tricks and one day he just quit."

"Got smart, I'd say," Dallas grumped.

"Could be," Dad said, as if it didn't matter. "Any way you slice it, we win. With HARP finished for the summer, it'll come in handy to have a few days' board. Besides, I wouldn't say no to a friend of Maxine's."

"It's nice that we're fixing up the corral for them," Sam said.

Dad nodded. Out by the spare corral, Pepper and Ross were brushing their hands together as if they'd just finished up.

"Brynna says the snow's gonna have a high moisture content this winter," Dad said. "That makes it real heavy. Reinforcing those fence posts now is work we won't have to do later after a heavy snowfall breaks it down and our stock goes wandering."

Sam sighed. Everybody thought the movies were no big deal. Dad wouldn't spend more than a few minutes talking about Inez Garcia and her horse.

Maybe haying was to blame, Sam thought as all four men loaded up and drove away. Cowboys avoided work that wasn't done from the saddle, and haying was the worst.

Once the men had left and she was alone with Ace, Sam couldn't help talking to him.

"As soon as you've met Bayfire, I'll take you out

and let you stretch your legs," Sam said as she threw the gelding's reins over the hitching rail near the house.

"You suppose he'll act like a regular horse?" Sam asked Ace. "Or like a movie star? Not that I've ever met one, and I guess Inez Garcia doesn't qualify, but how cool would it be to earn your living by working with trick horses?"

If Ace felt any of her fizzing excitement he gave no sign of it. He just sniffed the ground for something to eat, as she thought of how Inez Garcia and Maxine Ely, Jake's mom, had met at a teacher's conference five years ago. That was before Inez left the classroom to help her father run Animal Artists, a business that trained and managed movie animals.

According to Jake's mom, Inez specialized in equines. She handled mules, burros, and even a performing zebra, but Bayfire was her favorite. Sam could picture the horse in her mind, because she'd seen a photograph of him in a horse magazine as he was presented with a Trigger Award.

In the black-and-white shot, Bayfire had looked like the champion he was. He'd stood alert with his poll flexed and ears pricked while his owner and trainer, a slim, pony-tailed woman, had accepted the glittering trophy.

The short article had explained that Bayfire had received the award not only for his ability as an actor, but for a sense of contained energy that electrified the screen. One of the presenters had saluted his ability to show a spirit "like fire in a bottle."

Now, everything stood ready for the Hollywood trainer and her famous horse.

About ten minutes after Dad and the hands departed, Sam heard the sound she'd listened for all morning.

Wait. Maybe it was the drone of that small circling airplane. No, there it was. A dark-green truck slowed for the bridge over the La Charla River and drove so carefully, Sam heard the clunk of every rotation of each tire.

Sam smiled, already liking Inez Garcia. Someone who was that careful of the horse she was hauling was Sam's kind of person.

Ace turned his head and considered the vehicle. His ears flicked back, his eyes flashed with suspicion, and he raised a rear hoof.

"Stop that," Sam chided him. "This is a movie star stallion."

The gelding lashed his tail and kept staring.

From the ten-acre pasture, Strawberry snorted. Amigo and Popcorn eased closer to the fence, but the other horses accepted the quiet arrival of the strange vehicle with a quick glance.

Sun glazed the truck's windshield so that Sam couldn't see inside very well. She made out the driver's outline and the glint of sunglasses, but that was about all.

Sam pushed her auburn hair back from her face and tried to neaten it with her hands. If she'd gotten all dressed up this morning, her family would have noticed and teased her about it.

So, she'd pulled on clothes fit for cleaning the barn, and now it was too late to worry about what she looked like. She picked some straw from her shirt and stomped her boots to displace the layer of gray dust.

If Inez Garcia really wanted to be where no one would fuss over her, Sam thought as the green truck stopped, she'd come to the right place.

Trying to ignore her sudden shyness, Sam straightened her shoulders, lifted her chin, and started toward the truck. She'd taken only a single step before she stopped.

Inez Garcia might not be a movie star, but she was beautiful. The woman easing out of the truck must be close to six feet tall. She wore slim-fitting jeans and an open-necked white shirt. Her black hair was gathered high in back and silver hoop earrings danced in her ears.

Inez Garcia jerked her sunglasses off. She stuck them in her shirt pocket as if she wanted a closer look at everything. Her eyes swept over Sam, feinted toward Ace, touched on each building and pasture, and returned to Sam. Then, Inez Garcia smiled.

"Hi," Sam managed as the woman came closer.

"I'm Samantha Forster."

"I'm so glad to meet you," Inez said. Despite her exotic looks, she sounded pretty normal. "It's not a long drive from Alkali where the rest of the crew's set up, but I was afraid I'd miss the turnoff."

"A lot of people do," Sam said. "When I first moved home from San Francisco, I'd forgotten about landmarks. I didn't know how to give directions without talking about cross streets and exit signs, but you found us."

Stop blabbing, Sam scolded herself, but when she heard hooves shifting in the trailer, she couldn't help adding one thing more. "It sounds like Bayfire's ready to get out."

A shadow swept over Inez Garcia's face.

"Ms. Garcia, did I—is something wrong?"

"No. Of course not. And please call me Inez." She drew a breath. "Nothing's wrong. In fact, your ranch is lovely and I'm sure Bayfire will be quite comfortable here. It's not home, where he shares the stable with a mule, two burros, and a zebra, and he has his own paddock with a view of the San Gabriel Mountains, but he needs a change. And this"—she nodded toward the sun-streaked Calico Mountains— "is far different."

"I bet," Sam said, but she wasn't thinking of Bayfire. River Bend Ranch must seem pretty dull to someone who owned a zebra. Sam felt like she should apologize. "I'm sorry no one else is here to—"

"This is perfect," Inez assured her. "In fact, if you have something else to do, please go right ahead. Just explain where you'd like me to put Bayfire, then we'll settle in on our own."

"That corral is for him," Sam said, pointing past Tempest and Dark Sunshine. The buckskin and her foal stood at quivering attention. "I'm sorry it doesn't adjoin his stall—"

Sam broke off. Why couldn't she stop apologizing?

"Really," Inez said, laying a warm hand on Sam's arm. "We are very low-maintenance guests and grateful for the quiet. Don't give us a thought."

Inez glanced up at the sound of the small white plane overhead. For an instant, she looked even more distressed.

Sam wished she could figure out what was worrying the trainer.

"I see your horse is saddled," Inez said. She fidgeted a little, clearly eager to be alone.

"We're going out for a ride," Sam said. "Ace needs some exercise, but—I don't mean to be pushy, but do you think I could see Bayfire first?"

"Of course," Inez said, but she didn't sound flattered, and her manner was so competent as she unlatched the trailer door, Sam didn't even try to help.

"Back," Inez said.

On command, Bayfire made his appearance. As he backed down the ramp, the stallion's haunches gleamed. Sturdy, graceful black-shaded bay legs ended in white hind socks. He wore no halter, but his ears were cast back, listening for Inez's voice.

"Reverse," Inez ordered, and the horse turned to face them.

"He looks like Ace," Sam blurted. Then, at the astonished expression on Inez's face as she followed Sam's eyes to the little bay mustang, Sam added, "Well, a pumped-up version of Ace."

Bayfire had the thicker neck and broader chest of a stallion. His black mane and tail were full, but his red bay coat was no more burnished than her horse's. Bayfire's forehead wore a white star, too, just like Ace's.

"There is a resemblance," Inez said, slowly.

Why did the woman sound like she was just being generous? Inez must see the horses' similarities.

"Forward," Inez said, and the stallion took two steps ahead until he stood between them.

The stallion was incredibly obedient, but the precision of his movements bothered Sam. The beautiful horse moved like a robot.

"Ace is a mustang," Sam said, to cover her uneasiness.

"Is he?" Inez's head tilted slightly as she studied Ace. "Bayfire is Andalusian and Thoroughbred."

"Wow," Sam said, and she meant it, but the stallion's noble bloodlines didn't make up for his dreary expression. Bayfire looked nothing like the fiery horse in that Trigger Awards photograph.

Something was really wrong. That must be why Inez appeared to be holding her breath.

And since Inez knew what was best for her horse and obviously wanted to be alone with him, Sam said, "Well, I guess I'll mount up and—"

Just then a gaggle of Rhode Island Red hens came clucking from the direction of Gram's garden.

At the sight of the fluttering, muttering hens, Bayfire was a horse transformed. His neck arched until his chin bumped his chest, and Sam saw a glimmer of the horse he really was.

"I'm not sure he's ever seen chickens before," Inez said with a chuckle, then rushed to give the horse a cue to release him. "All done."

Right away, the stallion shuffled nearer the chickens.

"Bay, what are those?" Inez crooned to the horse. "Do you like those chickens?"

Though they avoided his hooves, the hens didn't scatter. Clearly, they were stuffed with bugs they'd pecked up and swallowed in the garden, and they'd decided this horse wasn't much of a threat.

"We could get you some for stablemates," Inez went on. "Would you like that, Bay?"

But when the horse looked at her, he seemed to deflate.

His bearing was still showy, but the sparkle left his eyes. When he lowered his head, he didn't sniff the chickens. His head hung, as if he had no desire to hold it up.

Sam noticed that the saddle horses in the ten-acre pasture moved away from the fence. Ace closed his eyes and dozed at the hitching rack. Dark Sunshine had gone back to grazing. Only Tempest and the two humans still watched the stallion.

Bayfire wasn't acting like a star. Was he exhausted? Sick?

Sam caught her breath, and Inez made a small sound like a moan as a plump red hen centered herself between the stallion's polished front hooves and, totally unafraid, proceeded to take a dust bath.

Sam couldn't ignore the insult to the stallion.

"Is he all right?" she asked.

"Physically, he's fine," Inez said. "And, as you saw, he'll do anything I ask of him. But Bayfire just isn't himself. He's lost heart," she said with a sad smile.

Sam swallowed. What could she do? Maybe telling Inez about the Phantom's depression would help, but the Phantom had been injured and deaf. This was completely different.

No, Sam decided, she could only listen. She waited for the woman to go on.

"Talking with Maxine Ely made me hope Bayfire would . . ." Inez gave a self-mocking puff of breath. "This sounds silly, but I've been hoping he'd sort of find himself, out here on the range."

"It's not silly," Sam insisted. She knew just what the trainer meant.

Inez's hand hovered above the stallion's glossy neck, as if she were afraid to touch something so rare.

"I really hope he recovers. Because if he doesn't, his movie career is over."

Chapter Three ⌘

"*B*ayfire's not just . . ." Sam searched for a word. For a moment she could only think of *limp*, but then she said, "gentle?"

"This isn't gentle," Inez snapped. "This is practically dead."

Sam flinched. Then, as if that weren't enough, Inez rushed to demonstrate what the stallion had lost.

"Bay," Inez said. As the stallion's gaze shifted to her, she made a slight gesture — almost as if she were brushing a tendril of hair back toward her ponytail. The signal brought him toward her, limping.

"He *is* hurt," Sam gasped and she turned on Inez with a silent accusation.

Inez had seemed so kind, but maybe she wasn't.

She'd said Bayfire was in great shape, physically, that his lethargy was all in his head. What if she'd lied? What if Inez wanted Sam to get out of here because she treated the horse badly?

"I promise you he's not hurt," Inez said, gloomily. "That would be too easy."

"What do you mean?" Sam asked, and Inez must have heard her suspicion.

"Does that sound hard-hearted?" Inez asked as her expression turned melancholy. "It isn't, believe me."

Sam watched. It was as if the horse's condition actually pained Inez.

"Limping is one of his tricks," Inez explained. "So is acting ashamed." At another gesture, the stallion hung his head and rolled his eyes guiltily to one side.

"Oh yes, good boy, good boy." Inez praised the horse. With each word her hands petted and rewarded him, but the horse acted numb.

"Let's try neighing," Inez said. She swept her hand up her throat in a gesture so graceful, Sam expected the stallion to sing. He gave a whinny that was more croak than melody.

Still, Inez praised the stallion. "You are perfect, Bay, perfect."

She slid her hand lovingly under the stallion's mane, though the horse took no pleasure in it.

Sam tried to make sense of the stallion's reaction. Or lack of it, really.

She watched Bayfire's eyes. His gaze stayed fixed on the air. Even his eyelids didn't move. He didn't recoil at all. From working with Dark Sunshine, Tinkerbell, and Jinx, Sam knew flinching would have been swift and involuntary if Bayfire had been abused.

The horse was an actor.

Sam shook her head, telling herself it wasn't the same as a person being an actor. But still, she wondered. What if Bayfire was ignoring Inez on purpose, to hurt her feelings? Was that possible?

"He's had X-rays and ultrasounds on all four legs," Inez said.

"All four? He only limped on that leg," Sam said, pointing.

"That one leg, this one time," Inez agreed, "but he takes turns with them. He limps on whichever leg pleases him at the moment."

Sam remembered a story Dad or Gram had told her.

"Was Bayfire *ever* injured?" Sam asked. "We used to have a ranch dog that limped because he really liked the massage he got when my dad rubbed medicine on one of his paws."

"Again," Inez said wistfully, "that would make sense, but no. Despite all the special effects—all the explosions and plastics shattering around him—he's escaped injury. Always."

Suddenly, the trainer turned cool and professional again. Sam recognized the attitude shift, because she'd seen Brynna do exactly the same thing.

"All this talking is accomplishing nothing, and I'm delaying you," Inez said. "I'll put him in that corral."

"That's right," Sam said, though Inez hadn't asked which corral. "Make yourself at home. I'm only riding out for an hour or so, and I'll probably beat Gram and Brynna back from town. Dad and the hands won't be back 'til sundown." Sam tried to stop talking, but she couldn't. "So, you'll have the place to yourself, but if you're hungry—"

"I have a small kitchen in my camper," Inez finished for Sam. "You've been very hospitable, Samantha. Now, enjoy your ride."

If that wasn't a dismissal, Sam didn't know what was, so she swung into Ace's saddle and rode toward the bridge.

She only glanced back over her shoulder, once. When she did, she saw Bayfire, the movie star, following at his trainer' heels, no more fiery than a well-trained dog.

Sam didn't have time to brood over the stallion's melancholy, because Ace was being a brat.

The gelding fought the reins, disgruntled by her decision to keep him at a walk as they crossed the wooden bridge.

"Just ready to run, are you?" Sam asked, but her little bay gelding snorted, crab-stepped, and tossed his head.

"It's not like you've been neglected," she muttered

to Ace as he swung his front hooves onto the dirt on the far side of the bridge. "I'm allowed to have a life outside this saddle," she added when no amount of weight-shifting and leg pressure made him behave.

Last week, she'd worked at Deerpath Ranch with Mrs. Allen's grandson, Gabe, who was recovering from a serious car accident at the same time a colt from the Phantom's herd was recovering from an awful burn.

"So, you weren't worked for one week. For a really good reason. That's not such a big deal," Sam said, scolding the horse. Still, she was glad he couldn't remind her that the week before that, she'd spent most of her time at the fairgrounds during the rodeo.

Ace mouthed his bit and Sam sat hard into the saddle, hoping he'd get the message that it was not okay for him to bolt, though the open range was in sight.

His black tail lashed from side to side, stinging her leg through her jeans, but Ace didn't lunge into a gallop.

Sam patted his sleek neck in appreciation, then made a clucking sound. Ace swiveled one black-edged ear back to listen.

"Where do you want to go, sweet boy?" Sam asked the bay gelding once they were off the bridge.

Ace stopped. He lifted his head and listened to the La Charla River's rushing. Then his ears pricked left.

"You got it," she told him.

Sam leaned forward in the saddle, firmed her legs, and let the reins droop from their straight line to Ace's bit. As competent as Bayfire had been with Inez, Ace read her silent signal and vaulted into a gallop. Wind snatched Sam's hat from her head and she leaned her cheek against Ace's warm neck. It wasn't a full-out run, but the gelding was having fun, loving the breeze of his own making, savoring each scent filling his nostrils, stretching the strong sinews in his slender legs.

When Ace seemed willing, Sam slowed him. They loped alongside the river. Out in midstream, several boulders showed dry, sandy tops. The river was low. It would take that wet winter Dad had talked about to bring the water level back up.

While she rode, Sam thought of the listless Bayfire. Growing up on River Bend Ranch, she'd gotten to know lots of horses. Some of them, especially those in the HARP program, had had problems.

She thought of Dark Sunshine, trapped, tricked, and abused. The mare still hadn't recovered completely, but her wariness lessened each day and Sam knew the buckskin trusted her more than she had six months ago. Popcorn had been abused, too, but the gentle albino had responded to good food and kind treatment. So had Tinkerbell and Jinx. But she'd bet her saddle Bayfire hadn't been abused.

And if he'd been traumatized, like Firefly, the mustang colt who'd been burned in the brushfire,

Inez wouldn't be trying to guess what was wrong with the stallion.

At first Sam thought a bird had made Ace hop sideways in mock fear. Her teeth clacked together at his sudden movement, but she didn't lose her stirrups as she would have a year ago. By the time she'd resettled herself, she realized it wasn't a bird at all, but the same little white plane she'd seen earlier that morning.

What was going on with that plane, anyway? Sam glanced up in annoyance.

The plane waggled its wings.

Did the pilot see her? She hoped so, because he was skimming way too low over the range and he'd frightened a knot of red Hereford cattle into a reckless run.

Sam shook her fist skyward. Those were River Bend cattle! She'd helped gather them herself. She didn't want them panicked. What if a calf became separated from its mother and ran over a dropoff, or into a gully and broke its delicate neck?

What an idiot, Sam thought. The pilot pulled up then. He banked toward the Calico Mountains. Wisps of dust blew, but Sam didn't think they'd been stirred by the plane. There, by the stairstep mesas, dust drifted like smoke amid the high tangles of pinion pine and sagebrush and suddenly, on the ridge top, Sam saw a horse.

It could be the Phantom.

Or maybe another horse, she told herself, trying to be sensible.

Someday she'd spot the mustang stallion when she had binoculars in her saddlebags, but today she had neither binoculars nor saddlebags, so Sam dropped her knotted reins over the saddle horn.

"Just give me a minute, Ace," she said, then pulled at the corners of her eyes, trying to improve her vision.

The pale blur that might have been the Phantom was just coming into focus when the plane zoomed overhead and Ace spooked again.

Did the pilot think this was his own private recreational area, or was he looking for something?

"Glad to see you go!" Sam shouted as the plane finally flew on toward Alkali.

Sam and Ace were nearly to Three Ponies Ranch and Sam was mulling over what Inez meant when she'd said Bayfire wasn't himself, when Ace's lope slowed to a hammering trot and his head swung right.

In the quick silences between Ace's hoof beats, Sam heard an equine snort. Someone was over there.

She found Jake sitting on the riverbank. He lifted one hand in greeting, but he didn't look at her. His eyes stayed fixed on the silvery river rills as the water found its way around the rocks.

So, what else was new? Actually, Jake's stillness was sort of a relief. Unlike the half hour she'd just spent with Inez Garcia, Sam didn't have to work to figure out why he was acting the way he was.

Jake had settled here on the riverbank and become part of his surroundings. That was just Jake. And he wasn't a chatty guy. Ever.

Witch, Jake's black Quarter Horse mare, leaned forward to touch noses with Ace. Well-trained and devoted to Jake, she stood ground-tied nearby.

"Hi," Sam said.

Beyond the tumbling, gurgling waves, she heard a magpie's call and saw a flash of black-and-white feathers.

"Hi," Jake said.

And because she knew he'd tell her to keep on riding, if he didn't want company, that greeting was as good as an invitation to stop for awhile.

Without shading his eyes, Jake squinted up at Sam as she dismounted. Jake wasn't wearing his hat, but something else was different.

Something was making him look older and more serious. Suddenly, Sam realized what had changed.

Jake Ely had cut off his hair.

Chapter Four &

Sam forced herself to look at Jake more closely.

He hadn't cut it *off*. Not even short, really. It still grazed his shirt collar, but no strip of leather bound the thick hair that was the same night black as Witch's gleaming coat.

"Got somethin' to say?"

Sam shook her head, but Jake wasn't fooled.

When he actually had the nerve to laugh at her shock, teeth flashing white, she wasn't a bit surprised.

"Why, Samantha," he teased with the phony drawl he knew she hated. "You're as quiet as a horse thief at a hangin'."

Sam plopped into the sand a few feet away from

him. Deliberately, she leaned over and looked out at the river, just like he'd been doing. If he thought she was going to burst into the outraged reaction he seemed to be fishing for, he was out of luck.

"It's *your* hair," she told him.

"Darn right," Jake said.

Sam realized they were both sitting up with their arms crossed, though, deadlocked.

Sam really did want to know why he'd cut off the hair that seemed—at least to her—like a symbol of his Shoshone heritage. If only he didn't have that teasing gleam in his eyes.

No way, she thought again. She would not give him the satisfaction of believing she was taking this more seriously than he was.

"It's no big deal, Brat," he said.

"Who said it was? It'll grow back."

"Uh-huh," Jake said.

But Sam's curiosity was like an itch. The longer she ignored it, the worse it got.

She ordered herself to wait an entire minute before asking a single question. Because she wasn't very good at patience, she decided to count to sixty.

One, two, three . . .

Ace's hoof, clacking against a river rock as he moved toward the water, distracted her.

Four, five, six . . .

Sam's fingers gathered into fists, but she concentrated on the creaking of saddle leather as Ace lowered his head to drink.

Seven, eight, nine . . .

Sam tightened her crossed arms, trapping her fingers against her ribs instead of looking at Jake, who pretended he was on the verge of dozing off.

Ten, eleven —

Sam focused on Witch as the black mare walked over to join Ace. They drank quietly, as if they weren't really thirsty.

Then, suddenly, the words came tumbling out of Sam's mouth.

"Did your mom make you do it?" She demanded.

Jake gave a "gotcha" laugh.

"Mom suggested it," he admitted. "Since I'll be talkin' to folks about scholarships."

"Okay," Sam said, releasing a sigh.

"Glad I got your consent."

"Shut up," Sam told him, but she was smiling as she leaned back against her hands and lifted her face to the sun.

Now she remembered. Before school started, Jake and his mother were taking a road trip to visit colleges. Nevada only had three four-year colleges, but they were going to check out a couple of northern California schools with good agricultural programs, too.

"You'll be back in time for the BLM auction, right?" Sam asked.

"'Course," Jake said.

It was a good thing, Sam thought, because Brynna expected the two of them could help the Bureau of Land Management wranglers sort the wild horses that were available for adoption.

"I'm not leavin' for a year," Jake said, and Sam wondered why he'd suddenly jumped ahead. "I might not even go to college."

"Don't say that," Sam told him. "You've been saving money for college ever since I've known you."

Jake stared past her, filling his eyes with the brown ridges that soared against the blue sky. He gave a slow shake of his head.

"I could get there and hate it."

"You need to go to college," Sam insisted, but he wasn't listening to her. He was studying his horse.

"Maybe you'd like to have Witch while I'm gone," he said.

Have Witch? Take Jake's horse? A panicky pulse pounded in the side of Sam's throat, but she just said, "She's too much for me, Jake. You know that."

"Couple hours in the saddle and she'd know you were the new boss."

"Yeah, well, it's that 'couple hours in the saddle' part that would slow me down," Sam said.

Jake smiled. "You could handle her."

"Yeah, right," Sam said. Sam glanced at Witch and for once the black mare's ears pricked forward in anticipation, instead of flattening in annoyance.

"Why do you talk like you're not brave?" Jake asked.

Sam's head whipped around from watching Witch.

Brave was an awfully solemn word, but Jake just stretched as if he'd gotten a kink in his back sitting there at the riverside.

"I'm *not* brave," Sam said.

Some dangers had crossed her path, sure, but usually when she stood firm, it was to help a horse. And for each time she'd faced a threat, there were two times she'd hidden or used her head.

Jake weighed her protest, then said, "Well, if you're not, at least you're stubborn."

"Like I haven't heard that before," Sam said with a laugh.

"Stubborn can make you determined," Jake told her. "Sometimes, bravery and determination can take you the same place by the end of the day."

"Just remember you said that," Sam told him, but she felt uneasy.

Jake's out-in-the-open honesty—about college and about her—felt weird. And he'd cut his hair. Maybe the three years' difference in their ages really did count.

"Can we quit talking about this?" she asked.

Jake gave a short laugh, probably because she was always trying to pry more words out of him, not fewer.

She watched Witch and Ace in the river. Ace pawed at a leaf swirling on the river's surface, then stopped, hoof still raised. Water dripped from the wispy feathers at his pasterns. Sam pictured Bayfire, thinking that every extra hair had been trimmed to give him a sleeker look.

Bayfire. She hadn't said a word to Jake yet about the stunt horse.

"Hollywood crew at your place yet?" Jake said.

Sam knew she should be used to it by now. How many times had Jake's careful observations and tracker's instincts made it seem like he could read her mind?

"Not the crew, but Bayfire and your mom's friend Inez."

"So?" Jake asked.

"So, she's gorgeous and smart and loves her horse, and he's—" Sam paused. Of course the horse was beautiful, but that hadn't been her strongest impression of him. "Jake, his trainer's right. There's something wrong with him."

"Like . . . ?" Jake encouraged her.

"Like, if I knew, I'd be a Hollywood horse psychiatrist."

Sitting here with Jake, Sam tried to be more sensible about Bayfire. The stallion could just be feeling lazy.

"I promised Mom I'd go check him out, but tell me what he's like," Jake said.

"Beautiful, half Andalusian and half Thoroughbred," she said. "He has amazing conformation, sleek but powerful, and a mane and tail so full, you'd call them bushy, if they weren't so well-groomed. But he does seem kind of burned out."

"Mom thinks he's shot so many scenes on some studio lot in Hollywood, he's sick of pretending."

And Jake must think there was a possibility that was true, or he wouldn't have mentioned it, would he?

Even though she was surprised, Sam didn't rub in the fact that Jake was always teasing her about imagining horses had human feelings.

"Hey, so why are they shooting it here? Do you know what the movie's about?" Sam asked.

"Mom's got this idea we'll get starstruck if she tells us too much," Jake said.

"Oh, right," Sam chuckled. She couldn't think of any guys less likely to turn into groupies than the Ely brothers.

"All I know's TriMax Studios is bringin' one horse and some cameras—"

"But is it, like, an Old West movie, or a story that's supposed to take place in, I don't know, Switzerland or something and—" Sam broke off when Jake tilted his head to one side. "Okay, keep going. I'll be patient."

But Jake didn't keep going. He glanced up as if he were looking for the little white plane that had been creasing the sky all morning, but it had disappeared.

As usual when she was patient, Jake finally went on.

"The movie's 'working title'—which means it could change, I think—is *The Princess and the Pauper*."

"That sounds familiar," Sam said.

"It should. It's a takeoff on Mark Twain's *Prince and the Pauper*, only since Violette Lee's going to be in it—"

"Wow! Really?" Sam sat back as if she'd been pushed, then closed her mouth when she realized her jaw had actually dropped in disbelief.

Having a stunt horse at River Bend made some kind of sense, but Violette Lee was a rising young actress who'd been in lots of cool movies.

Sam didn't really know much about her, but she could picture Violette Lee's yards of satiny blond hair and her delicate hands darting in little fairy movements.

Wait, her memory needed to be updated, Sam realized, because she was picturing Violette from a TV show she'd starred in as a little girl.

"What was the name of that show she used to be on, Jake? Violette played Santa Claus's youngest kid," Sam reminded him, but Jake was pretending he didn't know. "Come on," she urged. When Jake rolled his eyes at her excitement, she jabbed him with her elbow. "Jake, I can tell you know. What was it?"

"Why didn't I let you keep on ridin'," Jake

grumbled, but when she continued watching him, patiently, he added, "It was called *Meet the Clauses* or *Everyday is Christmas* — something like that."

"I loved it," Sam said, although now that she thought about it, it was a mystery that the program, which showed how Santa Claus's family spent the rest of the year, had lasted more than a season.

"So does *The Princess and the Pauper* take place during, you know, knighthood days?"

"If you mean during the medieval period," Jake corrected with mock patience, "yeah."

"So they'll be putting the horses in armor and Violette will probably be wearing big poufy skirts," Sam said as she imagined the scene.

"Don't talk to me about the costumes and sets," Jake ordered her. "Because I've heard enough. I was barely awake this morning when I heard Mom instructing Dad in all the ways Hollywood botches history. I bet he was late for work."

"Well, history is her thing," Sam said, though it was funny to imagine little blond Mrs. Ely following Jake's towering dad around, lecturing him like she would a student.

"I wonder why they'd shoot a medieval movie here," Sam mused. "We're kind of short of castles."

"Only one scene," Jake said. "I guess they shot most of it in a studio in Hollywood and at a movie ranch down there, but they're shooting a waterfall scene in Lost Canyon."

"What waterfall?" Sam asked. "There's no—wait. You mean that place where the trail seems to dead-end into that big rock face and there's this little, teeny trickle of water?"

"That's it," Jake said. "They're going to"—Jake made a vague gesture— "digitally manipulate pictures of water so it looks like it comes roaring down, something like that. I don't know, really. Ask Nate. He gets it."

Sam pictured the top of that rock face. She'd never ridden up there because a clear and level trail ran along its base. Now that she thought of it, though, there was a notch at the top and water might be seeping down from there.

"I'm sorry you'll miss it," Sam said.

Jake shrugged.

"This turned out to be the best time to go college shopping, as Mom calls it. We should have gone last year during spring break, but Mom didn't push it because Grandfather wanted me to do all that stuff."

"All that stuff" meant the week she, Jake, and his grandfather Mac Ely had captured and gentled a wild pinto filly at Monument Lake. Sam was kind of surprised that Mrs. Ely, a teacher, would let the prime time for visiting colleges pass, but maybe she'd figured Jake's experience with his grandfather and the filly Shooting Star had been a different kind of education.

Even though Jake didn't look very disappointed,

Sam decided he must be, so she tried to cheer him up.

"I wish you could at least spend some time with Bayfire. You'd do him good."

"That's part of the plan," Jake said. "When my mom heard Inez was coming, she started looking for really low plane fares and found some. We can leave here later if, after we drive to the college in Reno and check it out, we fly to the one in Las Vegas.

"Great!" Sam said.

"Mom'll get to stick around and tell movie people what they're doin' wrong and I"—Jake pretended to touch the brim of his cowboy hat, though it sat in the sand beside him—"will be right here to help you with that horse, little lady."

Sam doubted Inez was about to turn Bayfire's rejuvenation over to two kids, but she couldn't resist teasing Jake.

"You're just full of yourself, aren't—" Splashing made Sam break off and glance toward the river. "Witch! What are you doing?" Sam called after the horse.

Sam bolted to her feet. The black mare was trotting upstream.

Jake flashed Sam a frustrated glance as if he couldn't decide which of them was the most irritating—Witch, for wandering off, or Sam, for asking the horse why.

"I'm not gone yet, you addle-brained mare," Jake said. He rose slowly to his feet, speaking sternly but quietly, so the horse wouldn't bolt.

Ace raised his muzzle from the river, too, and finally Sam and Jake heard what both horses had.

Someone was calling for help.

Chapter Five ❧

"Go!" Jake said. He gave Sam a shove between the shoulder blades, which propelled her crashing through the shallows toward Ace.

She snatched up a single rein as it trailed past.

"Get going," Jake called over his shoulder as he pursued Witch. "I'll be right behind you."

Ace rolled his eyes at the jerk on his bit, and swerved toward Sam. Jogging, she led her horse up the riverbank.

"Good boy," Sam told the gelding, but his front hooves were shifting as she mounted. Her boot barely touched the stirrup as she vaulted into the saddle.

Sam heard Jake and Witch behind her. The Quarter Horse mare breathed loud with excitement.

Ace was running before Sam's heels grazed his sides.

Some distance ahead, maybe a couple of miles, the small white plane sat on the range.

Had the plane crashed? For one cruel minute, Sam wondered what the pilot expected when he went flying around chasing range cattle, but she shook off the thought.

Sam and Jake let the horses gallop, pushing them harder when an arm-waving figure appeared alongside the plane. Ace responded with a leap. The clatter of his hooves drowned out all other sounds. Had she ever ridden him this fast before?

Sam molded herself to her horse, leaning down on Ace's neck. His blowing black mane whipped stinging against her face. She was so determined to ride out this two-horse stampede, Sam barely noticed when her short-legged gelding thundered past Witch.

Through eyelashes squinted against the wind, Sam saw the figure leaning against the plane. Wait a minute. No flame showed orange against the desert. No smoke billowed. And that person looked almost relaxed.

She couldn't run Ace at this speed much longer if it wasn't a real emergency. Sam moved her fingers on the reins. It was a tiny movement, but Ace's reaction sent his weight slamming back on his haunches. His hindquarters tucked under. His head rose and Sam caught her breath, trying not to lose her seat as Ace skidded to a dusty stop.

Sam looked back. She couldn't believe she'd left Jake and Witch so far behind. They approached at a swinging lope, though Sam could tell by the way Witch shook her head from side to side that it was Jake's choice not to gallop.

The black mare wanted to catch up with Ace, but Jake had apparently reached the same conclusion Sam had. This wasn't a rescue.

So why had someone yelled for help?

Sam couldn't quite catch her breath, which was ridiculous since she wasn't the one who'd run across the range flat out. Then she realized her hat had flown off her head and lay against her back. Only her stampede string, pulled tight against her neck, had kept her from losing her prized brown hat.

Sam put her hat back on. Then, still steadying it with one hand, she yelled, "Are you okay?"

Distance blurred the answer, but she heard enough to know the person leaning against the plane was female.

The first words Sam made out were, "Until your hat fell off I thought you were a cow*boy*."

While the remark was irritating, the lilting voice told Sam the person standing before her was Violette Lee.

She didn't look like she had in the sitcom. No dramatic fall of silken hair hung to her waist. Instead, her pinkish-peach hair stopped at her chin, divided into hanks, as if it wasn't very clean. Her face was pale, but not much of it showed beyond her huge sunglasses.

It didn't seem likely that she'd been yelling for someone to save her. Still, by the condition of her rumpled jumpsuit, which was cut in a military style but printed to resemble snake, crocodile, or some other reptile's skin, she could have been here a while.

"Admiring my flight suit, are you?" Violette asked. "Well, I'm admiring your horse. What a wonderful little runner!"

As the actress rushed forward, hand lowered for Ace to sniff, he champed his bit and splattered her with foam.

"Yes, he is. A fine runner, and the sweetest, most slobbery boy, too."

In the middle of the desert, on a Friday morning, Violette Lee was babbling baby talk to Ace.

The whole situation was so unreal, Sam's brain had trouble catching up with what her eyes were showing her. Sam swiveled in her saddle to meet Jake's eyes as he reined Witch to a stop. In the shade of his black Stetson, which of course had stayed on his head, Jake's expression was impossible to read.

"My flight suit," the actress repeated, and her voice sharpened as she looked up at Sam.

"Uh, it's nice," Sam answered.

Really, though, it wasn't. In fact, the ugliest garment Sam had ever seen was hanging off Violette's collarbone and the little points of bone atop her shoulders.

"D'you scream for help?" Jake asked. He bumped the brim of his hat back, and now that Sam could see his face, he looked so clearly unimpressed that he had to be faking it.

A faint smile lifted the actress's lips, but Sam couldn't tell if it was for Jake or Witch. Violette kept one hand curled around Ace's sweaty neck as she reached toward the black mare. Amazingly, Witch didn't bare her teeth, and when Violette spoke, she cooed as if she were talking to the horse instead of answering Jake's question. "It's open country, and I thought it might be the quickest way to get transportation."

No excuses, no playing the damsel in distress, Sam thought. It had been a trick to make someone pay attention. Instead of getting mad, though, Sam marveled at the way Violette Lee, the world-famous actress, tolerated the sweat and saliva of the horses, just to be near them.

Sam tried to put the facts together. Had the plane crashed? Was the pilot sitting inside the cockpit, injured or trying to fix whatever had gone wrong?

"Is your pilot okay?" Sam asked.

Pulling away from the horses as if it pained her, the actress drew herself up tall.

"I am the pilot," Violette said flatly.

Rather than making the point that Violette Lee

was a bold adventuress, the statement made Sam mad.

Violette had been the one buzzing the cattle, Sam realized. Though she wanted to, some mental road-block kept her from scolding the actress.

"I'm also Violette Lee," she said, in case they hadn't noticed. She reached a tiny hand up to grasp Jake's. "But you can call me Vi."

Sam waited for Jake's blank look to fade into infatuation. How could he *not* develop an instant crush? Violette Lee was one of the hottest movie stars around and she was, well, flirting with him.

Jake didn't speak. He didn't smile, or even nod.

Jake gave Violette's hand a single perfunctory shake and released it so quickly, her reptile-patterned sleeves might have been hiding a real snake.

He must be faking it, pretending he wasn't starry-eyed under the brim of his hat, Sam thought.

But then Jake lifted his reins and backed Witch a few steps away.

Sam wanted to tell him he was being rude. She wanted to make it up to the actress. She also wanted to know why Violette Lee had landed in the middle of River Bend Ranch, when the scene she'd be in probably wouldn't be shot for days.

"Vi . . . ," Sam began.

"You can call me Miss Lee," the actress corrected.

She must be kidding, right? Sam gave a nervous laugh.

"No joke, dearie," the actress said. The honeyed voice that had crooned to the horses had turned cold. "Now, I'll need one of these horses."

What? The question slashed through Sam's mind. She wasn't sure if she'd said, or just thought it.

Jake backed Witch another step farther away.

"Oh come now," Violette said, chuckling. "I can handle that beautiful creature. Don't think I can't."

"Nope," Jake said.

Sam was amazed. Jake didn't even pretend to apologize.

"Truth be told, I get along with animals far better than—" She lifted one bony shoulder in a gesture that Sam took to mean everyone else.

Sam believed it.

Seeing she wasn't getting anywhere with Jake, Violette exhaled loudly and turned to Sam. "I suppose your mount will have to do, then."

Not Ace. She didn't let just anyone ride Ace.

"I don't know," Sam said slowly.

Half her mind told her to refuse. The other half reasoned that if Bayfire was here to do a stunt for *Princess and the Pauper*, and Violette was starring in the movie, she probably did know how to ride.

So why was she hesitating? Not just because Violette was a stranger. If Inez Garcia had asked to borrow Ace, Sam knew she'd hand over the reins without a word. But Violette Lee was bossy and temperamental. Ace would pick up on that and who knew what would happen.

"Let's go now. Out of the saddle and turn over the reins. Quickly," Violette said. She didn't snap her fingers, but her icy tone indicated she didn't expect to be delayed much longer.

Sam looked helplessly toward Jake.

All her years of reading his silence were no help. She had no clue what he was thinking.

Sam was about to give in. After all, it was the polite thing to do, wasn't it? She couldn't ask Violette to drive her plane up to the bridge, and walk over it to the ranch yard, could she?

Actually, it wasn't a long walk, and the actress wore thick-soled footwear that looked like motorcycle boots. Still . . .

And then Sam saw Gram's car coming and relief washed over her.

"Here comes your ride," Sam said, pointing.

Violette glance over her shoulder at the yellow Buick, then turned back to Sam with a sigh.

"I don't think so," Violette said.

Was it possible she was too cautious to hitch a ride with a stranger?

"No, really, it's okay," Sam assured her. "That's my grandmother and stepmom."

"Lovely," Violette said, and though there was no way she was misunderstanding Violette's snobbish tone, Sam noticed Violette blushed and pushed up her sunglasses as if she could hide behind them.

Then she crossed her arms.

Seeing them gathered there, Gram braked to a stop. When she did, the car's engine stopped running. Sam really hoped Gram had turned it off. The Buick had been stalling a lot lately, and though it took no more than a push to get it going again, that was the last way she wanted to welcome Violette Lee to River Bend Ranch.

"Hello," Gram said as she climbed out from behind the steering wheel. She wore a pale-blue dress and her gray hair was tucked into a tidy bun. If she thought this was as weird a situation as Sam did, it didn't show.

Brynna wasn't nearly so unruffled.

"Is everything all right?" Brynna asked, but when Sam recognized Brynna's expression, she braced herself.

Her stepmother had shifted into biologist mode, and as she looked at the crushed vegetation in the plane's path, and smelled the fumes from its engine, Sam would bet Brynna was thinking that somebody better have a pretty good excuse for the damage.

"Brynna, Gram, this is Violette Lee. You know, the actress?"

Violette extended her hand to Gram, giving the same faint smile she'd used to greet Jake. It said this was just another boring part of being a celebrity.

Brynna raised one reddish eyebrow. She'd been

kind of moody since she'd been pregnant. Right now, Brynna looked as if she felt insulted.

Surely Brynna wouldn't say anything mean, would she?

She didn't, until they'd all shaken hands.

"There's an airstrip at Gold Dust Ranch, just one ranch over," Brynna pointed out.

"I saw it," Violette responded, smiling.

Uh-oh, Sam thought. Here it comes.

But Brynna didn't argue with the actress. Instead, she tried to educate her.

"Barren as it looks, the high desert ecosystem is quite delicate," Brynna said. "If you should fly in here again, you'll want to use it."

"Well, no," Violette paused.

"I should have said, you'll need to use it," Brynna explained.

She might be dressed in maternity jeans and a loose-fitting blouse, but Brynna also wore a sense of authority.

Sam saw the actress part her lips, shift her jaw to one side, then press her lips into a line as she sized Brynna up.

Then Violette flashed an overly sunny smile. "Of course," she said. "And if it wouldn't be too much trouble, I would so appreciate a ride out to that little farm." Violette nodded toward River Bend. "I believe someone's waiting for me."

That little farm?

Brynna's face flushed dark red, and Sam realized her own cheeks were ballooned full of air. Gradually, she let it out as Gram rushed in to say, "Of course, and we hope you'll stay for dinner as well."

This time, Violette actually blushed a little. Gram was such an expert at guilt, Sam thought. She hadn't had to point out that it was her ranch to make the actress feel embarrassed.

Violette drew a breath and wore an expression that looked like real regret.

"Sorry, but I can't stay. I'm just stopping in to see how Bayfire is doing."

That fits, Sam thought. Judging by the way Violette had acted with Ace and Witch, she was a fanatical horse lover. Being worried over Bayfire— worried enough that she'd make a crazy landing without an airport—made a kind of sense.

"Is Bayfire here?" Brynna asked Sam. "And Inez Garcia, too?"

Sam nodded and would have said more, except that Violette hadn't stopped talking.

"That horse is quite dear to me," she said. She gave a helpless shrug as if she wished it weren't so. "He was my mount in *Redcoat's Daughter*, of course, and we got on together so well, I requested him for *Little Sure Shot*."

Sam swallowed, hard. No one said anything, and it was obvious they never got off the ranch to see a movie. They hardly ever even rented videos.

Sam gave a hum of appreciation, but Violette's mocking laugh said she wasn't fooled. She shook her head as if she'd never seen such a bunch of ignorant bumpkins.

Chapter Six ❧

"The car's engine died when we stopped," Brynna said bluntly. "I'll hold the horses while you help push."

For a second, they all stared at Gram's old yellow Buick.

"All you have to do is get it rolling," Gram said. "Once you do, I can pop the clutch and we'll be off." She headed back to the driver's door.

Violette didn't offer to help.

Sam hadn't really expected her to, but it would have been nice.

Putting her hand against the sun-hot fender of the yellow Buick, Sam guessed that it probably wasn't Violette's fault. It was like professional athletes, Sam thought, as she braced her legs and leaned all her weight against her hands. They were treated like kings because of their physical skills, not because they were smart or kind or interesting.

Even though Jake pushed, too, the car moved only inches at a time. The strength of another person would have helped.

"On the count of three, give it all you've got," Jake said, glancing over at Sam. "One, two—"

"Three!"

Sam and Jake gave one last shove together and the car began rolling. As Gram popped the clutch, the Buick started. Sam glanced over at Violette, who was examining her hair for split ends.

Gram stopped the car just a few yards away, then gunned the engine.

Brynna gave both horses pats before handing their reins back to Sam and Jake. Then she turned to Violette. She took a deep breath, released it, and Sam could tell Brynna was trying to backtrack and be nice.

"Shall we go?" Brynna asked. She still sounded stiff, but she was making an effort.

Violette wasn't. While Brynna waited for her to get in, the actress stood outside the car with one hand on the roof. Cautiously, she peered inside.

With the manicured index finger of her other hand, she pushed her sunglasses up her nose, then splayed that same small hand over her chest. She swallowed almost as if she felt a little sick, but she got into the car.

Brynna gave a disbelieving laugh at Violette's lack of gratitude. Then she looked back at Sam and threw her a kiss.

As the Buick drove away Sam asked Jake, "What was that for, do you suppose?"

"Compared to her," Jake said, nodding after the car that carried Violette, "I guess you come off looking pretty good."

"That's not very hard," Sam said.

Jake took his hat off and smacked it against his leg, getting rid of the dust clinging from their headlong gallop to Violette's nonrescue.

"Never thought you'd turn Ace over to an incompetent rider," Jake snapped.

"I didn't," Sam said, though guilt crashed down on her like an ocean wave. "And what makes you think—?"

"We were just talkin' about this," he said, gesturing back toward the river. "You usually stand your ground. Why were you givin' in to her? Because she's rich and famous?"

"No! I'm interested in the movies. I want to know more about how they make them, and how they train the horses and stuff," Sam said, but Jake's accusation hurt.

She hadn't done anything wrong. Still, she had been about to let Violette ride Ace, even though it made her uneasy. And she could learn more about movie horses from Inez.

"Later," Jake said, before she could decide what to say, but he didn't turn Witch toward home. He rode right after Gram's car, toward River Bend.

The black Quarter Horse moved at an easy lope and Ace wanted to go after her, but Sam didn't mount up. She stood staring after them, thinking.

If Jake was mad at her and disgusted by Violette, why was he going where they were? It took Sam almost a minute to remember what Jake had told her down at the riverside. He'd promised his mom he'd take a look at Bayfire.

Jake's destination didn't have a single, solitary thing to do with her.

The first thing Sam heard when she reached home was Violette complaining. Maybe because she'd heard the voice on television, years ago, the whining sounded familiar.

"Seriously," Violette said, "what kind of godforsaken place doesn't even have cell phone service?"

Violette paced along the fenceline of the ten-acre pasture. No humans stood near her. As far as Sam could tell, the actress was talking to Popcorn, who plodded along listening from the other side of the fence.

The albino mustang watched as Violette strode toward the chicken coop.

"I must arrange for a lift out of here," she muttered, "before I allow myself a visit with my sweet Bayfire."

"Could she be talking to the chickens?" Sam whispered in disbelief to Ace. As if he were pointing out that she was asking this question of a horse, Ace just continued toward the hitching rack.

So did Violette, holding her phone at various angles, and now she was snarling under her breath.

What should I say to her? Sam wondered, but then Gram appeared on the porch.

"Would you care to come in and use our real phone, dear?" Gram asked.

Once more, Violette looked faintly chagrined at Gram's kindness.

"Thanks," she said, and followed Gram inside.

Which personality was Violette's real one? The warm-hearted animal lover or the cold-blooded snob?

Sam swung down from the saddle and tossed her reins over the hitching rail, then followed the direction of Ace's alert ears. Together they watched Inez brush Bayfire in the small pasture. The trainer rubbed the stallion's already glossy coat with long, smooth strokes, massaging more than cleaning.

Why hadn't Inez come up to greet Violette? Surely she'd noticed her.

Sam hooked her stirrup over her saddle horn and leaned down to loosen Ace's cinch.

"Well, I'll tell you what," she told her horse, "I'm staying out of the way until someone decides to include me."

She might go looking for Jake, though. If he thought she could be swayed by someone just because that someone was a movie star, he didn't know her at all.

"I was only being polite," Sam explained to Ace. "That's it. Really."

She took her time cooling out Ace and picking packed river mud from his hooves. Then she began brushing sweaty, loose hair from his coat.

She was humming a country-western ballad to her horse, and had almost forgotten Violette when the actress came out of the kitchen and let the screen door slam behind her.

That is so weird, Sam thought. *Violette Lee just came out of my house. She's walking this way. What should I say to her?*

It turned out Sam shouldn't have worried. Violette passed close enough to let Ace sniff her hand, then kept walking toward Inez and Bayfire.

"She could have said something to indicate she'd passed another human being, too," Sam muttered to Ace. "But still, it is kind of cool that she's here."

As Sam watched, Inez gave Bayfire a pat on the rump, sending him toward the box stall, then turned to talk with Violette. For a minute the actress just stared after the horse, but then she straightened and faced Inez.

Sam couldn't help eavesdropping.

"Finally," Violette said, giving a dramatic sigh, "someone's coming out from the little encampment at Alkali to give me a ride back to the plane. When I flew over, it didn't look like there was much there. In the town of Alkali, I mean. Just two buildings, and they count that as a town? You could say I'm doing them a favor, breaking the boredom."

"*You* could say that," Inez answered, though her tone sounded as if she didn't agree.

Sam couldn't imagine having someone drive twenty miles round trip from Alkali, just to save yourself a half-mile walk.

As Violette went on, Sam noticed Inez just murmured in response. She must have discovered that was the safest way to deal with a temperamental star.

"You know my agent doesn't want me flying," Violette boasted, "but he can't stop me, so he wouldn't let TriMax put it in my contract." She waited, then gave an impatient shrug before adding, "That I couldn't fly during the making of the movie."

Inez murmured again, and didn't seem surprised when Violette followed her toward the open box stall.

Holding her basket of grooming tools, Sam trailed a few feet behind them until Inez looked over her shoulder, smiled, then used her head to motion to Sam to catch up. Irritated by Inez's attempt to include Sam, Violette grabbed the trainer's arm and tugged her close to ask, "How's Bayfire? He looked fine, but—"

"He *is* fine, Violette, and I know why you're here."

"It's no secret," Violette said. "We've finished most all the studio work on *The Princess and the Pauper*. As a gift to myself, I decided to fly out to visit you and my favorite horse in the world."

Even though Sam couldn't see the actress's face, she could imagine she'd be wide-eyed and a little hurt that Inez thought she had another motive.

"That, of course," Inez said, but then she threaded one finger through the end of her pony tail and twirled it like a girl. "But there's one other thing."

"I don't know what you mean," Violette said, looking puzzled.

"Honey, it's not happening," Inez said, kindly. "TriMax doesn't want you doing your own horseback stunts. And that *is* in your contract.

"We're out here in Nevada solely to do stunts," Inez continued, "and we only have three days to get Bay ready and the scene shot. I don't have time to fight you on this. You're not riding Bayfire through his performance." Inez sounded firm, but understanding.

Violette gave a squeaky groan.

"But you know what a good rider I am and how silly that is," Violette insisted.

"I do, but your contract is invalidated if you break that clause," Inez said. "Your agent told me himself in the strongest possible terms. He said he'd see to it you never worked in another movie with me, if I allowed you to ride Bayfire in a stunt."

Violette rushed into the barn ahead of them. Sam caught her breath as the actress unlatched the stall and left the door standing open while she hugged the stallion.

Bayfire stood quietly, accepting the embrace.

Inez bent to retrieve the actress's fallen sunglasses from the straw, then said, "I can't let that happen, Violette. You two are such a good team."

Violette kept her face buried against the stallion's mane as she answered Inez.

"I'm in love with Bayfire, and the only time I get to be with him is when we're making movies." Then she looked up. "My agent is nuts," she said with a sniff.

When Inez showed no sign of changing her mind and left the barn, Violette crossed her arms and followed. "I don't know why you won't sell him to me."

"Because I love him, too," Inez told her. "And he helps pay the bills."

"That's so wrong," Violette said. She pretended to pout, but Sam wasn't sure if it was because Inez wouldn't sell Bayfire or because Inez made her living from the horse.

"How are Rudolph and Cupid?" Inez asked.

"Getting old, but fine," Violette said. "And don't think you can change the subject and distract me. They're nothing like Bayfire. Besides, I'm allowed to have two reindeer and still want a horse."

Chapter Seven ๑ง

Reindeer? Sam was about to ask how the actress had come to own two reindeer when Violette began smooching toward Bayfire.

When Violette called his name, the stallion went to her.

Did Violette just know how to summon the trick horse, or did Bayfire really like her? Sam couldn't tell. The stallion stood quietly while she stroked and cooed to him, but his eyes didn't leave Inez.

At last, a tan SUV drove into the ranch yard.

It must be Violette's ride back to her plane, Sam decided as the actress gave Bayfire a final hug.

Then, from the corner of her eye, Sam saw Inez bob her head as she had earlier today when she'd told the stallion he was all finished with his tricks.

Could Inez have used a silent signal to call the horse to Violette, just to make the actress happy? Or was it a business ploy, used to let Violette think the stallion liked her?

Violette tousled her hair with one hand and held out her other hand for her glasses. Once Inez returned them and she'd slipped them back on, Violette hurried toward the waiting SUV.

Poised with one foot on the ground and the other inside the vehicle, Violette turned and waved as if a cheering public were seeing her off. Once Violette had closed herself inside the vehicle, Inez said, "She didn't need to come here."

As the tan SUV drove away, Jake appeared from the tack room. Had he been there all along?

"Can I check him over?" Jake asked Inez.

"Sure," the trainer said. Then, with a glance after the SUV, she added, "All of Vi's work was shot in and around Hollywood, but she's one of those actresses that falls in love with her costars. If they're animals."

Inez and Sam watched Jake feel Bayfire's front legs. He looked up, about to say something, and Inez interrupted.

"I hope you won't judge our entire industry by Violette."

"Of course not," Sam said. "Besides . . ."

Sam stopped talking when she felt Jake staring at

her. Did he think she'd been about to make excuses for Violette? So what if she had?

Jake gave a sarcastic snort, then looked surprised at himself.

"Sorry," he said. He stood slowly, trailing his hand over the stallion's shoulder.

"She really does care for Bayfire," Inez admitted as Jake continued to examine the horse. "And it's not unusual for actors to fall in love with the horses they ride and want to buy them. Directors and trainers discourage it, though," she said with a sheepish smile, "partly because the actors end up wanting to do more riding than the script calls for. Even if they're good riders, every minute on the horse puts them at risk. An injured actor can stall the entire production, and delays equal dollars."

Sam thought of all the makeup, camera, and props people employed to make a movie. They probably had to be paid, even if they were waiting around, so that they wouldn't take another job and not be available when the actress recovered from her accident.

And on television, you always saw microphones hanging overhead and cords snaking around. All that equipment had to be expensive, too. She could see why directors wanted to minimize risks.

"Besides that, Violette has some issues," Inez said bluntly. "I get along with her as well as anyone does, and even I worry about her emotional condition."

Violette was beginning to remind Sam of the HARP girls.

With a final pat, Jake left the horse, then the stall, closing the gate behind him. After latching it, he sank his hands into his pockets and cleared his throat. When he finally talked, he sounded ashamed.

"I didn't mean anything by bein'..." He shrugged, and though he didn't complete his apology, Sam guessed he was talking about his sarcastic snort. "I wasn't so polite out there," Jake said, nodding toward the range.

"Don't worry," Inez said. "Violette's got a thick hide. She doesn't make a secret of her problems, either. Quite the contrary. I'm sure when she comes back, she'll share the secrets of her difficult childhood."

"You really think she'll come back?" Sam asked.

Forget Jake. He could think what he liked about her.

"Yes, even though I've asked her not to. Her curiosity won't let her rest until she knows what's going on with Bayfire," Inez said.

"You mean, what kind of stunt you're going to do with him?" Sam suggested.

"That," Inez agreed, "and Violette's sort of an animal activist, too."

"Mom mentioned her arrest," Jake said.

"Arrest?" Sam gasped. This was more and more like having a HARP girl on River Bend. The only difference was, this troubled girl made millions of dollars each year.

In answer to Jake's statement, Inez held up three fingers.

"She's been arrested three times?" Sam said, staring toward the range. Although she couldn't see the small plane, she heard its engine snarl into action once more.

"Three I know of," Inez said, hinting there had been even more. "She broke into a pet shop and stole all the animals. And I mean all—puppies and kittens from dirty cages, guinea pigs that she thought were overcrowded, and feeder mice that were waiting to be fed to pet boa constrictors."

"I didn't know," Sam said. "It seems like I would have read about that."

"She didn't go to jail or anything, because the judge was sympathetic. He ordered Violette to pay for damages to the building, but he also made it his business to see that the pet store owner was investigated and the owners fined for their violations."

Sam felt a grudging respect for Violette, which had nothing to do with her acting ability. She was kind of like an avenging angel for animals.

"She also broke into a tropical fish store and 'rescued' some fish that had supposedly been injected with dye to make them more colorful," Inez said.

"Supposedly?" Jake asked.

"A few had," Inez said. "But hundreds died in

transit to their new home and an innocent employee—who'd already reported the abuse—actually got a serious electrical shock when he slipped in the huge pool of water Violette and her helpers left behind. He fell on one of the damaged aquarium heaters."

"Who were her helpers?" Sam asked.

"Teenage fans," Inez said, grimacing.

"Just goin' along with her 'cause of who she is," Jake put in, and Sam knew the remark was pointed at her.

"Whatever the reason," Inez said, "it meant she was charged with contributing to the delinquency of minors and that, plus the electrocution, didn't make her look good when she pulled her last rescue."

"Guide dog for the blind," Jake mumbled.

At least, Sam thought he said that, but the image that created—of the actress dognapping a service animal—was impossible, wasn't it?

Sam faced Inez, but she couldn't bring herself to ask for the truth.

"Violette thought the dog's owner was too bossy," Inez said, raising her palms skyward.

Too bossy, Sam thought. And this was the woman who'd ordered Sam to hand over her horse.

As if talk of Violette's problems had made her more able to face her own, Inez suddenly nodded toward Bayfire.

"What do you think of my boy?" Inez asked Jake.

"I'm no expert," Jake began.

"Don't be modest," Inez snapped. "Your mother said you're a natural with horses and Brynna Olson—that would be your stepmother?" Inez asked Sam, and she nodded. "Seconded Maxine's opinion."

Inez Garcia obviously didn't like turning to kids for help, Sam thought. She must be pretty desperate.

"He looks healthy," Jake began.

"Totally," Inez agreed. "As I told Samantha, he's been gone over by experts, and he still does everything I ask him to do, but he used to love it. He doesn't anymore."

"Could he be bored?" Jake asked.

"I don't see how. The special effects, the different costumes and makeup for each movie . . ." Inez shrugged. "The work is ever-changing. That's what attracts most of us to it. Bay faces new challenges in each performance. And he's not showing signs of exhaustion, either."

All three of them stared at the beautiful horse.

"Makes you wish you could ask him what's wrong, doesn't it?" Sam said wistfully.

"Not really," Inez said. "Whatever it is, I'm pretty sure he blames me."

Suddenly, Inez seemed anxious to drop discussion of her troubled horse.

"If you'll excuse me, I need to get cleaned up," Inez said.

As the trainer went to her camper to get ready for dinner, Sam stared after her.

"I wonder what makes her think her horse is mad at her," she mused, aloud.

"We'll find out at dinner. Mom's coming over. They're havin' their little reunion at your gram's kitchen table while all the guys who've been haying have a spaghetti feed at our house."

"All the guys except you, right?" Sam asked.

"Yeah," Jake's tone asked if she wanted to make something of that.

Sam didn't. In fact, she was glad Jake was here to give his opinion of what might help Bayfire. But since Jake was already irritated, she figured there was no harm in reviving their earlier squabble.

"So, are you really mad at me for just being polite to Violette?"

When Jake didn't answer, Sam pushed harder. "Or maybe it's not me. Maybe you're disappointed because Violette Lee isn't the beauty she looks like in the movies."

Sam had noticed he'd looked the actress over, carefully.

"I don't care that she has a face that looks like biscuit dough and dresses in toad skin," Jake snapped, "and her attitude's her own business. What I can't stand is the way you let her boss you around!"

"Oh, so *her* attitude is her own business, but *my*—"

"You know what I mean," Jake said.

"Yeah, I do, and it's bad enough that you're overly protective of me when you think I might hurt myself, but what makes you think you can tell me how to act, too?"

Jake shook his head.

"That's what you're trying to do," Sam goaded him. "Right?"

"Why d'you want to give in to someone like her?"

"It's okay if I give in to you, though," Sam said, and finally Jake seemed to have had enough.

"Hey," he said. "You only need to put up with me for a couple of days. Then I'm out of here. And when I get back, it's not like we see each other that much at school. This time next year, I'll be out of your way for good."

She'd been mad enough to tell Jake he couldn't leave soon enough to suit her, until that last part. She'd hate it if Jake moved away permanently.

Since she didn't know what to say, Sam gave Jake a shove.

"Wait. I need to show you two something."

Sam and Jake turned at the urgency in Inez's voice.

When she climbed down from her camper, her eyes were red from crying.

"If this movie's going to be made with Bayfire in it, we don't have time for me to waste time being touchy. If you're going to help, you need to know the whole truth. Most of all I'm worried about Bayfire, but I'm also worried about myself. I'm pretty new to Hollywood, but so far I've got a dynamite reputation.

That can change overnight if people start thinking of me as the woman who wrecked Bayfire."

Neither Sam nor Jake spoke.

Sam didn't know about Jake, but she felt out of her depth with Inez's confession.

"So, why are you asking us for help?" Sam asked, and though her words came out in a near whisper, Inez understood.

"Don't take this the wrong way," Inez said, with a lopsided smile, "but I've tried everything else and now, well, I've got nothing to lose." The trainer cleared her throat loudly and went on, "Let me show you why I think he's mad at me and not just bored."

Sam looked over at Jake. He'd made some kind of little sound, something between a growl and a worried whine. Then he rubbed the back of his neck, newly bared by his haircut.

"Is this gonna be safe?" he asked.

"Safe enough," Inez said. Her black brows arched and she looked a little insulted.

"I trust you to know your horse," Jake said, looking down at his boots, "but I saw my dad and grandfather use a pitchfork to get a stallion off a man once and well, ma'am, I'm not set up for doing that before dinner."

Inez looked amazed. Then, she gave a giggle.

"Not before dinner?" she asked, before breaking into outright laughter.

Sam joined her. It was such a Jake thing to say, and of course he had no idea why it was funny. He just sighed.

"Hysteria," Inez explained. "That's all it could be, because this isn't the least bit funny. The horse I've loved since he was foaled hates me."

Sam didn't believe it was true, but as Inez called the stallion to follow her, then opened the newly restored pasture gate, Sam tensed.

Vaguely, she'd wondered why Inez had kept Bayfire in the barn instead of loosing the stallion into the pasture. Now she'd find out.

"Go play," Inez said, releasing the stallion from her control.

Even in the setting sun, the horse's coat shone with copper glints. Muscles slid smoothly beneath his glossy hide.

As Bayfire relaxed, Dark Sunshine snorted. She used her shoulder to bump Tempest away from the fence, but the filly ignored her and raced up and down, trying to gain the stallion's attention.

At first Bayfire hardly noticed, but when she whinnied in her newfound volume, he had to stare. Fearful of the male attention fixed on Tempest, Dark Sunshine acted, flashing her teeth, flattening her ears, and forcing her baby back.

"She doesn't take no for an answer," Inez said. "She won't hurt the filly, will she?"

"No," Sam said, "but Dark Sunshine's only a

couple years off the range and she still kinda goes by those rules."

"Rules?" Inez said.

Though Sam was eager to see the demonstration of hatred Inez had promised them, she explained, "Lots of the time stallions kill the foals of their rivals."

"That's right," Inez said, nodding. "I've read about that. I guess she can't take a chance. I wouldn't."

For the first time since his arrival, Bayfire struck out in a showy gait, performing for Dark Sunshine.

"Look at that," Sam said. "He looks better to me." When Inez didn't smile, Sam asked, "Does he to you?"

"For the moment," Inez said.

They watched as the stallion quit parading and lowered himself to the ground. He rolled, kicking his strong legs while showing his vulnerable belly. Finally he stood, shook, and blew breath through his lips.

"Now watch," Inez said. She touched her index finger to her temple and though the stallion clearly saw her, he turned away.

"Bayfire," she said, then touched her temple again.

He walked toward her stiff-legged, begrudging each step. Still, he obeyed.

When he was within six feet of the fence, his robot walk changed. His brown eyes rolled white, like a shark about to attack, and then he came straight at Inez, mouth agape, teeth aimed to rip her flesh.

He slammed into the board fence with such force, Sam wondered if it would hold. It wouldn't have if Pepper and Ross hadn't just renailed it.

In just a few seconds, though, the attack ended. The stallion trotted away, shaking his black mane.

"I don't think it's you," Sam started.

Inez pressed the heels of her hands to her eyes, then dropped them and glared at Sam. "What?" she demanded. "Do you think he was after the fence?"

"No, but—"

"I think Sam's right," Jake said.

"Then I'm afraid neither of you can help me. Whatever's wrong is between me and this horse," Inez said, and her voice held both irritation and regret.

"He's charging you all right, but if I went out to— well, watch this," Jake said. He hurried back to the barn, snatched up the first lead rope he came to, and approached the pasture.

"Don't go in there," Inez warned.

"I won't have to. Watch." Jake climbed to the second rung on the fence and leaned forward, dangling the lead rope. "Gonna getcha," Jake said playfully. Bayfire wheeled, arched his neck, pranced in a fiercely threatening manner, then bolted toward Jake.

Once more, his eyes rolled white and his black

edged ears, so like Ace's until now, flattened against his head. This time, he swerved before he struck the fence.

"So what have you proven? That he hates everybody?" Inez demanded.

"I don't think so," Sam said. "Maybe he hates leaving the pasture, and he's doing whatever it takes to make you let him stay."

Sam's words sounded so hollow, Inez didn't answer. Clearly, she hadn't shown Sam and Jake what she'd hoped to.

"All done," Inez said, flashing a sign to the stallion. Though she used words, she spoke as she would to a deaf person, depending on quick-fingered signals as much as words.

"Are you okay with leaving him out there while we eat?" Jake asked.

"I'm willing to do that, even though I shouldn't. Bayfire is a very intelligent horse and he's thinking about what earned him the right to do what he wants," Inez said.

The stallion looked cocky as he paced the perimeter of his new corral. He sniffed the top edges of the fence boards, then a patch of dry grass. In between, he stopped and tossed his forelock back from eyes that flashed a challenging glare.

The trainer was right. Bayfire's equine brain was used to learning. They'd just taught him if he acted vicious, he'd get his way.

"But when we return later," Inez said, "I'll need your help. Both of you."

"No problem," Sam said. "We should have lots of daylight left."

As they walked toward the house, Jake stopped at the pump to wash up.

"Give you two more room at the sink," he said.

Sam wasn't sure she wanted Jake to lag behind. She could feel Inez watching her, not as if she'd done something wrong, but as if she was wondering if Sam could be trusted.

"I know on a ranch you have a different relationship with animals than I do, but they still have to behave and bend themselves to what you require of them—perhaps cutting a calf out from a herd and putting you in position to rope it. If your Ace refused—"

"He has," Sam said, "and we've worked through it."

"But he's never charged you like that."

"No, Ace hasn't, but I think that's a stallion thing." Sam swallowed and looked toward the Calico Mountains. "There's this mustang called the Phantom . . ."

"Maxine told me you had a favorite colt that went feral."

Sam nodded. "Sometimes I'm still lucky enough to see him. And three times, when he's been under incredible stress, he's charged me like that." Sam stopped to take a breath, then said, "It's pretty scary."

"I've got to say, you don't seem as intimidated by it as I am," Inez said.

"It's a mock charge," Sam explained, feeling like an expert. "Wild stallions do it to weed out challengers who aren't worthy. When the young males are driven out of their home herds, it's one of the things they practice in their bachelor herds, and—"

"A mock charge," Inez interrupted. "If only it were."

They were almost at the house when Inez glanced back to see if Jake was still at the pump. He was.

Then, as Sam watched, Inez Garcia unbuttoned a button at her neck and lowered her white blouse to show Sam the top of her shoulder.

Black and purple bruising covered the top of the woman's arm, from back to front.

"He grabbed me with his mouth, lifted me from the ground, and shook me," Inez said quietly. "Samantha, there was nothing 'mock' about it."

Chapter Eight ❧

As Inez hurriedly adjusted her collar and smoothed her blouse back into place, Sam thought about the discolored flesh around the horse bite. Bayfire had inflicted that bite with crushing power. It was no nip and no accident. He'd lifted Inez off her feet.

"I see what you mean," Sam said. "He meant that bite."

"That's why I was sure something must be hurting him. I have been with this horse every day of his life for five years and he's never harmed me, not intentionally. My friendship with him was as strong as that with my best friend, with family! But something has changed."

The bump-bump of tires crossing the bridge made them both turn. As they did, they noticed Jake had left the pump. He was just a few steps behind them, giving a wave to the approaching car.

"Here's Mom," Jake said.

Since she had no advice to offer Inez, Sam was relieved when Mrs. Ely drove into the ranch yard, parked her Honda, and hurried over to hug Inez.

"It's so good to see you!"

Both women spoke in unison, then laughed and fell to chattering with such speed, Sam couldn't follow the conversation. Since it really wasn't her conversation to follow in the first place, Sam went inside and left Jake standing there, hands in his pockets, unsure what to do next.

"I was wondering when you'd come lend a hand," Gram said.

Though Gram was teasing, Sam hurried to help, setting the table with silverware and heavy pumpkin-colored napkins. Sam shuddered. The pumpkin-colored linen made her think of autumn, even though it was still summer outside.

In two weeks she'd be back in school. She liked school and was looking forward to seeing her friends, but why did she have to let go of summer?

She'd carried a huge wooden bowl of green salad to the table and poured glasses of milk or iced tea for everyone by the time Jake came in and stood fidgeting near the door.

When Brynna and Dad came downstairs, Gram said, "It's about time."

The screen door creaked as Jake leaned out to call, "Mom, they're ready to eat." Jake's mother and her friend crossed the porch with hurrying steps and Sam was amazed to hear Mrs. Ely giggling like a girl.

Gram put a cold platter lined with ruffled lettuce and layered with sliced ham and Swiss and cheddar cheeses on the table. She asked Jake to bring over a basket of bread she'd sliced off the morning's loaves, and a blue ceramic bowl full of pasta salad.

Sam looked at the table with approval. Almost.

It would have been a perfect summer dinner except for the sliced and steamed zucchini Gram had mixed with tomatoes from her garden.

Sam tried not to shudder. Plenty of times, she'd been told that she was too old to feel revolted by certain foods, but she hated cooked zucchini with tomatoes. Yuck.

And she knew exactly what she'd be told to do if she complained: take just a little.

While the adults talked about work, about the differences between city and ranch life and what Mrs. Ely and Inez had been doing since they saw each other last, Sam watched Jake. He'd taken lots of vegetables.

Quit acting like a baby, Sam told herself. At least the zucchini and tomatoes were sprinkled with toasted almonds. Using the silver serving spoon like a cutting horse, she tried to navigate around the zuc-chini and cooked tomatoes and take a scoop that was mostly almonds.

She looked up when Inez mentioned that after three years teaching eighth grade science, she'd taken on a job as nurse's aide, too.

"We only had a school nurse three half days each week," she explained, "so a couple of us teachers took up the slack. Mostly I was called on to diagnose sniffles and flu for kids who should've stayed home. And there were a few fakers, too, who showed up in the nurse's office to dodge quizzes and tests.

"For big excitement, there was the occasional P. E. injury. Dislocated fingers from basketball, bloody noses from slamming face first into the wrestling mat, twisted ankles from soccer, and a few broken bones from general fooling around. Actually, it was kind of fun."

"And yet you quit," Maxine Ely said. She didn't sound critical, Sam thought, just amazed as she added, "I can't imagine liking any other job the way I do teaching."

"Bayfire was born," Inez said helplessly.

"I remember your voice when you called to tell me," Jake's mom said. "I could tell it was love at first sight."

"Absolutely," Inez agreed, then turned to explain to everyone else. "Just after Bay was foaled, Dad got a call for a newborn foal to wobble around in a TV sitcom and he asked me to take Bayfire. Everyone on the set adored him and he was a natural in front of the cameras. The screenwriter wrote him into the script for six episodes and that took us to the end of the school year." Inez shrugged. "Dad's seventy-two and, uh, semiretired, so when he asked me to take charge of all the equines, I said yes. Since then, I've never looked back. It's the best job in the world. Most days."

Inez didn't have to tell anyone at the table that she was worried about Bayfire. They all knew.

"What makes your horse so special?" Gram asked. "Sam and Brynna tell me he's won some awards."

Inez considered the question for a second. "What makes him special is what's missing right now. There are lots of pretty trick horses—most of them white if they're ridden by stars—and lots of stunt horses. For those, they like bays or browns, so they can blend in and do their trick—falling is a big one in historical battle scenes—over and over again without the audience noticing it's the same horse."

"They do that?" Sam said, and just as she asked, she realized many times when Inez began discussing Bayfire, she veered away from his problems and talked about moviemaking instead.

"They do that, and they use computer generation," Inez said. "Usually when you see a huge battle scene with hundreds of horses, it was shot with a few dozen horses and then they're"—Inez moved her hand in a rolling motion, still holding her sandwich — "replicated. Don't ask me exactly how."

"Technology," Gram said, and the way she tsked her tongue sounded slightly disapproving. "But your horse doesn't need computers to help him look good, does he?"

"Bayfire can do almost anything," Inez said. "But actually, technology's helped movie horses. In the early days, horses were considered almost expendable."

Expendable. Sam turned the word over in her mind, not certain what it meant. It sounded as if you could spend them like dollar bills.

"In the old cowboy movies," Inez went on, "if they needed a horse to fall, they'd whip him into a gallop, then run him at a trip wire."

Sam caught her breath aloud.

"That's sickening," Brynna said. "They must have broken their legs."

"And necks," Jake added.

"Jake," his mother said, with a settle-down gesture.

"You're right," Inez confirmed. "Some horses died. I don't know if it's true, but legend says that at the end of filming the chariot races in that old movie *Ben Hur*, over a hundred horses had died or been destroyed."

"Since then, the humane societies have stepped in, haven't they?" Brynna asked. Inez nodded.

"They're on every movie set or they notify a local vet to show up and do a check. That helps, but so does intensive training."

"Like you've done with Bayfire?" Sam asked.

"Yes," Inez said briefly. "And of course there are special effects, makeup, remote control animal robots, and stuffies."

Sam realized she'd been so interested as she listened to Inez, she'd actually eaten some of the horrid vegetables. And she wasn't the only one who was fascinated. Dad leaned both forearms on the tabletop and Gram's sandwich lay half eaten on her plate. Sam wanted to kick Jake under the table and say, "See?" She wasn't the only one who wanted to know more about the movies.

"Robots I understand, but what are stuffies?" Mrs. Ely asked.

"Another Hollywood secret," Inez said, sipping her tea.

"Please tell," Gram encouraged her.

Inez sat back in her chair, head tilted to one side as she explained.

"Let's say the screenwriter describes a scene in which the horse has to slip on an icy trail and go hurtling down a mountainside. We might start with a stunt horse taking the fall, then cut in scenes of a life-sized stuffed model of a horse—sort of like a dummy—sliding down that hillside." She paused to be sure everyone understood. Sam noticed that even

Jake nodded. "So, we'd intersperse frames of the real horse acting like he's struggling, with pictures of the stuffie. It can look pretty realistic."

"Wow," Sam said. "Will you use those for this movie?"

"Sure. Those scenes have already been shot for *The Princess and the Pauper*. Oh, they used retractable swords and jousting lances, too."

"Retractable," Dad said, nodding. "Well, I'll be. So, when it looks like a horse is gettin' stabbed, really the blade's goin' back into the handle of the sword. Is that it?"

"That's it," Inez said. Her smile said she enjoyed showing off the mysteries of her business. "Add that to the convincing wounds you can make with morticians' wax and makeup and even though it's all illusion and harmless to the horses, it can look pretty realistic."

"But you still have to train horses to do things that run counter to their instincts, like slamming into those retractable lances," Brynna said.

"True," Inez said. "Some won't do it, but any movie horse has to, at the very least, answer his name every time, without fail, and follow hand signals in case there are loud special effects. Everyone's safety depends on that part of his training."

"We use lots of Quarter Horses for ranch work," Maxine said. "Are there any particular breeds you folks use most?"

"Thinkin' of startin' a sideline in movie horses, Mom?" Jake asked, and everyone laughed at his unexpected joke.

"Of course not," Mrs. Ely said, "but I *was* thinking of helping Grace clear the table. I guess I'll let you do that, since you've got enough energy to tease me."

Jake didn't complain, so Sam stood and helped him, but she kept listening so she could hear Inez's answer.

"My dad's always used Arabs," she said. "He likes to get them young, before anyone's messed them up, or breed them himself. He says Arabs will do anything once they understand what you're asking."

"And yet Bayfire's not an Arab," Brynna said.

"No, Bayfire was a magnificent experiment," Inez said, but in the seconds of silence that followed, the clink of Sam clearing silverware filled the kitchen and Inez's smile faded.

"Speaking of amazing horses," Gram said, suddenly, "Brynna and I saw some this morning in Darton."

Sam and Jake both stopped, as if they couldn't focus enough while carrying dishes.

"The school district's trying to open a small riding therapy center," Brynna explained.

"For kids like Gabe, who've been in accidents?" Sam asked.

"Gabe's the grandson on one of our neighbors," Gram explained to Inez. "He was in a terrible car accident that left his legs paralyzed. Thank goodness it wasn't permanent. Working with horses has helped him toward recovery. Now he's regaining movement in his legs—"

"Thanks to Firefly, his adopted mustang," Sam interrupted.

"And a riding therapy program near his home in Denver," Brynna added.

Sam welcomed the memories of Gabe and Firefly, but how could Gram and Brynna have known about this new Darton program, when she hadn't, Sam wondered. And why had they gone to check it out and left her behind?

"Actually it was Gabriel who got me interested in this," Gram said. "And then I talked with Amelia's grandmother."

"Amelia?" Jake's mother asked.

"One of the HARP girls," Gram explained. "Her grandmother wanted to buy Ace and donate him to a therapy program. It seems he's just the sort of horse they look for—bomb-proof is what they call them."

"That pony still has a few tricks," Dad said dubiously.

"*He* does, yes," Gram said. She tucked a strand of silvery hair back in her bun, and her eyes took on a determined look that made Sam a little worried.

"The Darton program will be for children with a variety of problems," Brynna explained. Sam couldn't help noticing her stepmother was looking at everyone except her. "Sadly, most of the conditions are longer lasting than Gabe's. But the horses seem to help with things like trunk control"—Brynna demonstrated by placing her hands on her rib cage and moving side to side as she might on a gentle horse—"cerebral palsy, things like that. The horses not only teach balance, but riders have to remember the process of putting on a helmet, how to put their feet in the stirrups, how to hold the reins—things like that."

Suspicious chills covered Sam's arms with goose bumps.

This was an awful lot of detail for Brynna to know without a purpose. And she couldn't be thinking about donating newly captured mustangs for this. That just wouldn't work.

When had Gram talked with Amelia's grand-mother? And why?

Sam glanced at Dad in time to see his sad expression.

"What sorts of horses do they use?" Inez asked.

"Kind, understanding horses," Gram said. "They have to be gentle with a rider who sometimes can't stay upright without volunteers walking on each side of the horse."

"In fact . . ." Brynna started, watching Gram as if she should finish the sentence.

Here it comes, Sam thought.

"In fact, I volunteered. Starting in September, I'll

be helping there two days each week."

Was that all? Gram was going to help out in the riding therapy program?

Sam sagged against the kitchen counter.

"I'll do the dishes," she offered, in relief.

And Gram took her up on it.

Chapter Nine ❧

"*I* think that's great, Gram," Sam said.

She looked over her shoulder as far as she could with her hands still in the sudsy sink, then smiled, so no one would suspect the twinge of selfishness she felt as she imagined coming home to an empty kitchen with no cookies and milk or, on cold days, cookies and cocoa.

Still, she agreed with Jake's mom when she said, "Grace, you'll be perfect. You're good with children and you know horses, but with all this"—Mrs. Ely's hands spread, indicating all the duties of running a ranch—"do you have time?"

"Lands," Gram said, shaking her head. "It will only be a couple of days a week, but I see a lot of plusses to it. After the baby's born, Brynna will want a little time for just the two of them—"

Brynna made a little sound of protest, but Gram kept talking.

"—and I feel like I still have something to contribute, old as I am, even if I do say so myself."

This time Sam turned quickly from the sink as she exclaimed, "Gram!"

She didn't think of Gram as being that old. It sounded like she thought other people thought she was useless!

"Your hands are dripping soapy water, Samantha," Gram said. "Be careful. We don't want anyone to slip."

"Somethin' to contribute," Dad said slowly. "Besides keeping the ranch accounts, payin' the bills, helpin' plant the crops, the garden, known' when to breed and gather livestock, and cookin' a few tasty meals along the way?"

"That's enough, Wyatt," Gram said. "Perhaps you and Samantha are right that I've no reason to feel at loose ends, but it just seems that Sweetheart and I aren't doing all we could. We have something to give outside our little ranch world."

Sweetheart? Sam was about to ask Gram what Sweetheart had to do with anything, when Inez spoke up and Sam realized the trainer had been listening just as attentively to this family talk as they had listened to her descriptions of the movie business.

"I think that's incredibly generous of you, Mrs. Forster," Inez said. "It would be a better world if more people thought like you do."

"Well, I don't know about that," Gram said modestly. "All I do know is that I have an angel food cake sitting over there, and strawberries sweetening, and if I don't hurry and whip the cream, everyone will be wanting to go to bed before we've had dessert."

Once they were full of the sweet summer dessert, they all walked out to the corral to see Bayfire.

"My reason for living," Inez said, dipping an arm toward the stallion.

"What?" Mrs. Ely yelped.

"What I meant was, my reason for living in my camper every time he's in a movie," Inez amended.

"Okay," Mrs. Ely said, as if that made far more sense.

"I'm still not exactly clear on what's wrong with him," Brynna said.

"He's not acting like himself," Inez said, repeating what she'd told Sam earlier.

Brynna gave a patient smile. "I'm a biologist and I guess that makes me sort of literal. What do you mean by 'he's not himself'?"

"He's bored, just moving through his behaviors by rote, and once in a while"—Inez paused, glancing at Sam as if she knew she'd remember the bite—"cranky."

"You told me that much on the phone," Brynna said. "I guess I'm wondering if you've worked up a training strategy to put the spirit back in him."

"I'm considering several things," Inez said, "but I'll take suggestions. You see, most of the actors' work is finished, but Bayfire's major stunt is still ahead. If that sparkle he's famous for doesn't show on film, the director may reshoot the scene with another horse."

"He looks lively enough," Maxine said.

Bayfire's eyes swept over them as they stood outside his corral. His ears and nose pointed at Inez, but he sidestepped and turned his head, as if considering the others from different angles would make them less of an audience.

He wasn't lively. He was concerned, Sam thought.

"Here now, nothing to worry about," Dad told him gently, but the furrows over Bayfire's eyes grew deeper and he looked even more anxious.

Even now, Inez wouldn't exactly focus on the stallion's attitude.

"Since our location manager spotted the perfect non-waterfall to shoot our jumping over the waterfall stunt," she said, pretending confusion, "I thought I'd take the next couple days to accustom him to the terrain and costuming."

"He has to wear a costume?" Jake asked

"Plastic armor, some caparison, you know, that

kind of fluttery skirtlike stuff you see on knights' horses in movies. He's learned to ignore smoke and explosions, cameras, and swords, so that's no problem."

"Really?" Brynna said. "I'm impressed."

"In *Redcoat's Daughter*, he had to strut in a manner that suited the arrogant general on his back, then carry Violette—playing the general's daughter—through a war scene, and find her on the battlefield after she'd fallen."

"I remember that! And that was your horse," Maxine Ely said. Admiration filled her voice, even when she added, "Though there were some historical inaccuracies—not your mistakes, of course—it was a really touching scene. It makes me tear up just thinking about it."

"Thank you," Inez said. "And though I give Bayfire most of the credit, please do tell Violette when you see her. She had a bit to do with it."

"I want to see that movie!" Sam said.

Jake gave a sarcastic moan.

"It wouldn't do you any harm to watch a quality movie," his mother said.

Jake shook his head, not about to quarrel like a kid in front of witnesses, but Sam could almost read his mind. She'd bet he was thinking of Violette's rudeness, her rumpled hair and clothes, and wondering where "quality" fit in.

"Anyway, before we try jumping him over the place where they'll computer-generate the trickle into a roaring waterfall, I need to work with Bayfire. I'm hoping to shake him up a little and remind him who he really is."

"If anyone can help you with that, it's these two. I know they're just kids, but to lots of people, not just their biased parents, they are horse wizards," Mrs. Ely said.

Jake looked at his mother in astonishment and Sam could only grin.

"Okay," Inez said, and Sam noticed there was still a reserve in her voice. "My plan is to relax him and work on a little muscle conditioning."

"And socialization," Jake put in.

Sam frowned at Jake. Couldn't he tell Inez didn't want to talk about Bayfire acting vicious?

"What's that about?" Brynna's voice was mild, but Sam saw her stepmother tense up.

"It's not like he needs a party," Inez joked.

"Jake?" Brynna asked.

"He's been acting a little rough," Jake said, darting a look at Inez.

"And nipping," Inez admitted.

Though that was a huge understatement, Sam was glad Inez had owned up to that much. Brynna's knowledge of horse behavior might really help.

"How old is he?" Brynna asked.

"Five," Inez said carefully.

Nodding, Brynna turned to watch the horse for a few minutes.

"It's a male vice," she said finally, and Sam noticed her stepmother flashed a look at both Dad and Jake, daring them to contradict her. They didn't. "If they're raised with other colts, they usually get it out of their system. Or at least they understand the consequences."

"What do you mean?" Sam asked.

"If you bite, you get bitten back," Brynna said. "But, if it hasn't been a problem before, I'd guess something else is going on. What do you think, Wyatt?"

"Stallions this age get to thinking they need harems of their own," Dad suggested.

"But I keep him busy and he's incredibly well trained," Inez protested.

Brynna bit her lip and Sam could tell she was trying not to contradict Inez.

But Brynna's studies meant she linked most behavior—human and animal—with primitive impulses.

When Brynna crossed her arms above the bulge of her baby, Sam saw the "we'll wait and see" expression on her face. Brynna didn't believe training could overcome instinct.

Where was the Phantom?

As Sam lay in bed that night, staring at the swoops and bumps in her plaster ceiling, she couldn't stop thinking of the wild silver stallion who'd once been her own. Had those been dust wisps she'd seen along the ridge top that morning just before she'd seen Jake? Had they been stirred by the stallion and his herd as they climbed the stairstep mesas and hid in the pinion and sage thickets?

What if Violette's aerial acrobatics had stirred up the mustangs?

Maybe the Phantom would come to the river tonight. Sam shivered at the thought. Every moment she spent with the wild horse was a gift.

But the plane could have had the opposite effect, too. The snarling, swooping thing could have spooked the mustangs. The Phantom might have decided to elude the strange mechanical creature by returning his band to the security of his hidden mountain valley.

Sam rolled on her side and stared at her white curtains. The light wind billowing them inward was chilly.

Summer was ending. Wild animals usually came down from the cool mountains to graze the lower, warmer range in winter.

She didn't know the altitude of the Phantom's valley. She'd ridden to it, heading sharply uphill and steeply downhill, squeezing along a tunnel that cut all the way through a mountain. The horses had sought refuge there in all weather.

Of course it wasn't a magical place, even though it felt like it. She'd heard Gram talk to her gardening club friends about microclimates, though. Sometimes, due to air currents or something, one little piece of earth could be warmer than the land around it.

Sam yawned, but she wasn't sleepy.

She missed the Phantom. A lot.

Sam sat up in bed, pulled her knees against her chest, and circled them with her arms. She longed to hug the stallion's neck as she had when he was a colt. But he was an adult now, and wild, and if she could just sort out her thoughts, she had a feeling that he could help her figure out what was wrong with Bayfire.

The Phantom and Bayfire were stallions of about the same age. They lived in totally different worlds, of course. Still, what if Brynna was right? Maybe the nature of horses didn't change all that much because of where they lived.

A snort sounded outside. A stallion's snort.

Sam swung her legs out from under the covers. Her bare feet barely grazed the floor before she was at her window, pushing her curtain aside.

Be him, she pleaded silently.

She stared into the darkness, toward the bridge.

Nothing moved except the river.

She couldn't see much of the ranch yard from here, so she listened. She heard restless hooves and the snort came again.

It was probably Bayfire, tense and puzzled, on this first night in a strange place with unknown horses. Only Inez was familiar to him, and he'd decided she was no longer his friend.

What was the bay stallion thinking, Sam wondered.

Horse thoughts, about food and family? But Inez was his only family.

That's it, Sam thought, yawning. From birth, Bayfire had trusted Inez to be his herd leader, to feed him, protect him, and entertain him. Now he needed something else, something he couldn't explain to her, and she wasn't coming through for him.

Sam told herself to quit thinking in circles. Tomorrow, they'd get busy and change Bayfire's attitude, or at least his daily routine.

They'd start the morning with a hill ride for fitness and a trip to Mrs. Allen's hot springs for relaxation. For socialization, the stallion would have Ace and Witch. And, if they were lucky, the Hollywood horse would experience some nose touching over the fence with captive wild horses at the Blind Faith Mustang Sanctuary.

Sam blew her breath against the window. It was just cold enough to condense, and she used her fingertip to draw the outline of a horse. She couldn't see how well she'd done because her room was so dark.

He's not himself, Inez had said about her stallion, and Jake had accused her of the same thing. Maybe they were both wrong.

Maybe Inez was expecting the stallion not to act like a horse.

And maybe Jake, not her, was the one who'd changed.

Where did that come from? she wondered.

Jake had been her friend for as long as she could remember. Even though he could be infuriating, she could always count on him.

Before today, she might have told herself Jake didn't let his life get crazy. She'd often thought that was because he was the youngest of six boys. Since his parents had had five other boys to practice on before they got to him, he'd just turned out just right.

That might still be true, but he was acting different today, almost as if cutting his hair had changed him.

No, Sam thought, yawning, it had to be the other way around. Jake had cut his hair because he was changing. She wasn't sure she liked the difference, but going away would be a lot harder for him than it would be for her.

Her mind was too muddled to keep going.

Sam crawled back into bed and pulled up the covers against the night wind and closed her eyes.

Chapter Ten ✆

They didn't ride out early the next morning.

Sam, Jake, and Inez had been reviewing their plans for Bayfire for about an hour.

They sat wedged in Inez's camper with cups of tea and microwaved breakfast sandwiches.

"These are delicious," Sam said as she licked a gooey string of cheese from one finger. "But you can never tell my Gram I had it. Deal?"

"Of course," Inez said, then she smiled at Jake.

Sam loved the playhouse coziness of the camper with its bed on a shelf and mini kitchen, but Jake kept bumping his shoulders. He just didn't fit.

"So, here's what we've got to figure out," Sam went on. "What does it mean—in Bayfire's world—to be a stallion?"

"That's like asking, What does it mean to be a man?" Inez said.

"Right," Sam said. She squinted out the camper window at Dad and the hands, gearing up to go back to the hayfield once more. "Like, my dad—"

Jake gave a short laugh. "*You're* answering what it means to be a man?"

"Look, Jake," Sam told him. "I happen to have a perfect example. Really. Like my dad usually loves his job, because mostly it is cowboying. But right now he hates haying, but he has to do it to feed the cattle, and since he's selling some off as a cash crop, he has to do it to feed his family, too."

"Yeah?" Jake said, as if the example didn't make any sense at all.

Apparently Inez agreed with him.

"I'm trying to follow you, Sam, but you're confusing me. I understand the part about Bayfire having a job, but he doesn't have a family."

"Of course he does," Sam insisted. "It's you. You're his herd of one, and even though you're asking him to do something he doesn't want to do, for the most part, he's doing it."

"Okay," Inez said, though Sam could tell the explanation still hadn't clicked for her.

Jake was starting to get it. As usual, though, he kept quiet.

That didn't mean he stayed still. Jake jiggled one foot. He leaned back. He tried to link his hands behind his neck. He banged his elbow on a cupboard.

"In the wild," Sam explained to Inez, "a stallion's job is a constant battle, for food, for mares, and for territory."

"She's right," Jake admitted, but Inez looked at Sam and Jake as if they were speaking some Western dialect she couldn't understand.

"Is that all?" she asked.

Sam thought for a minute, and a revelation hit her.

"No, they have fun, too! They play in the river, roll in the dust or the mud, and run for the pure joy of it. If we give him today and tomorrow to enjoy himself, maybe he'll be ready to work the next day."

Inez rubbed absently at her injured shoulder and tilted her head to one side.

"Maybe you're right," Inez said. "At first his work was like play, but maybe that's changed."

Jake shot to his feet, hunching his shoulders and keeping his head low so he didn't bang it on the camper's ceiling.

"Chuck my idea outta the window if you like, but here's what I think," Jake told Inez. "He's a horse. Maybe he just needs time to act like one."

By the time they made their way out of the camper, Dark Sunshine and Tempest were neighing for breakfast.

Sam hurried toward the barn. Before they left to take care of Bayfire, she had to care for her own horses.

"Come and get it!" Sam called. Dark Sunshine and Tempest followed Sam's voice into the barn.

Sunny nickered her approval as if she could measure the extra half scoop of grain with her eyes, and barely noticed Sam locking the door that would have allowed them to go back out and keep Bayfire company over the fence.

Jake had Witch saddled and ready for the trail. He'd tied her where Bayfire could see her, and by the time Sam emerged from the barn, Jake had caught Ace and was leading him to stand beside Witch.

"Now you want me to saddle your horse," Inez said as she took Ace's saddle and bridle from Sam.

"Just to make Bayfire jealous," Sam said.

"Uh-huh," she teased. "Well, I think you're just trying to get out of a little work."

Bayfire watched Inez, though he pretended not to.

Sam looked over in time to see the stallion bob his head, then extend his neck, looking to make sure his eyes weren't deceiving him.

"Yes, it's true," Sam called to the stallion. "She's saddling another horse."

"Sam, that's embarrassin'," Jake said.

"Look," Sam retorted, "Bayfire might not understand what I'm saying, but he knows Inez is paying attention to Ace, not him."

"Next, you think I should go in and clean Bayfire's corral, right?" Inez asked as she picked up a rake.

"Yeah," Jake said, unlatching the corral gate. "He's not actin' aggressive, not like he was yesterday, but if he tries anything—"

"I remember," Inez said, but Sam knew Inez wouldn't use the rake against her beloved horse unless her life was in danger.

Eyes fixed on the stallion, Jake eased the gate open so Inez could enter the corral. The bay stallion saw her coming and trotted to the far fence. Then he turned his tail on her.

"Whistle while you work," Jake suggested.

"I'm a lousy whistler," Inez said, but she made a breathy sound between pursed lips and started raking.

Bayfire stamped. He swished his black tail and called to Witch, who flattened her ears in reproof.

So much for socializing, Sam thought, but Inez's part of the scheme was working.

Bayfire glanced back over his gleaming right shoulder. Inez ignored him. The stallion glanced over his left shoulder. Inez pretended she hadn't noticed.

Amazed, the stallion turned to face her, but kept his distance.

"Hey there," Inez said to the horse, and now she was raking nothing but dirt.

The plan was working perfectly, and when the stallion extended a forefoot as if he'd take a step, Inez leaned the rake up against the fence and stuck her hands in her pockets.

"This is really weird," she said. "It's like starting over again with a new horse."

It had been Inez's idea not to use Bayfire's name and to keep her hands in the pockets of her jeans so that she couldn't accidentally give him a signal.

"That's right, boy," Inez said as the horse came a step closer, "you're just a regular old saddle horse today, nothing special."

Sam gave a quick glance at Ace. He wasn't looking at her. He pulled against his tied reins and stretched his lips, hoping he had enough slack to catch a piece of straw that was blowing along the ground just out of reach.

A sniff made Sam look back at Inez and Bayfire.

The stallion had slung his head over her shoulder, and though she still kept her hands in her pockets, Inez rubbed her temple against the stallion's neck.

"It's like a reunion," Sam whispered to Jake. "He doesn't like being mad at her."

"He doesn't like being ignored," Jake corrected.

Still, they stared at each other and smiled. Step one had worked just fine.

As they rode past the house on their way out of the ranch yard, Gram called out, "Inez, would any of your crew members in Alkali like to come out here for dinner?"

"Thanks Mrs. Forster—"

"Please, call me Grace," Gram suggested.

"Thanks Grace, but there are only five of them, and from what they tell me, they've set up pretty comfy headquarters in Clara's parking lot. They're making field trips out to the spot in Lost Canyon where we're supposed to shoot, but other than that, it sounds like they're shoveling down chicken-fried steak, mashed potatoes with gravy, and all kinds of fresh cakes and pies at Clara's."

"Humph," Gram said, narrowing her eyes in a competitive frown. "That doesn't mean they can't drive out for a single dinner. I always have plenty."

"I'm sure the food isn't half as good as yours," Inez assured Gram. "They're just doing their part, trying to keep good relations with the folks in Alkali, in case we have to come back for a reshoot," Inez explained. "Some people don't like film companies moving in and stirring things up, especially in small towns."

"I haven't heard a single complaint," Gram said. "And I would have, if things weren't going the way they were supposed to."

"That's good, but I wouldn't blame them if they were glad to see us go. We have all these electrical cords and bright lights that can turn night into day, and we need places to park huge trucks and, well, even though the little store there doesn't have much of what they want, Clara does. So, by spending time and money there and showing people we can be nice instead of stereotypical Hollywood snobs"—Inez paused and shot Jake a smile when he loudly cleared his throat—"we can make sure we're welcome."

"That makes sense, I suppose," Gram said. "But please don't hurt my feelings by not coming to dinner yourself."

"I shouldn't impose a second night," Inez said. "Really, I have a little kitchen in my camper and I've trained myself to open cans and run the microwave."

"Do that, Ms. Garcia," Gram said, folding her arms and tapping her toe, "and you'll have gone past hurting my feelings directly to insulting me."

"Well, I wouldn't want to do that," Inez said with a laugh.

"Dinner's at six," Gram said, and then, just before closing the door, she called, "Jake, I mean you, too, of course."

"Yes ma'am," Jake shouted back over his shoulder.

Sam was smiling, feeling relaxed and cheerful, when Gram had to go and spoil her happy mood by adding, "After all, Jake, we don't know if we'll have you around here for dinner next August. This might be our last summer together, so we'd better make the most of it."

Chapter Eleven ❧

All day, they worked Bayfire up and down the mesas.

At first the horse was a little hesitant. He moved quickly and powerfully, but his head swung from side to side, scanning the ground behind boulders and stands of pinion pine.

Inez wore a dark-green baseball cap with her black ponytail poked through the back. Her hands were quiet on the reins and she tried to ride wordlessly, so that Bayfire wouldn't search her sounds for commands. But when the horse seemed to almost tiptoe, alert to the faintest flicker of birds' wings, her lips curved into a defeated smile.

Finally, Jake rode alongside Inez.

"What's he looking for?" Jake asked.

"Cameras," she muttered.

Sam barely heard, because she was riding ahead, but she turned in the saddle and watched.

It was weird to see a horse act self-conscious, but Bayfire definitely understood that all eyes were on him.

While she watched Bayfire, Ace picked their next trail.

"Not that one!" she gasped.

"What's up?" Jake called, before Sam had pulled Ace to a stop, her hands fumbling on the reins.

"Uh . . . ," Sam stalled. She wasn't about to tell Jake that if they continued up this dusty smudge in the hillside they'd pass through the tight stone tunnel she'd been thinking about just last night, the one that ended at the Phantom's secret valley.

With a scuff of hooves, Bayfire stopped, too. Ears on alert, forefeet clearing the ground, he pivoted on his hind legs.

"Uh," Sam repeated.

She tried not to squirm beneath Jake's stare. She was a bad liar, and a lot was at stake. Her best bet was to offer some version of the truth.

"I've seen wild horses up here," Sam said. She faced Inez and let Jake look at the back of her brown Stetson. "I'm not sure it would be a good idea for Bayfire to meet up with them. Especially with another stallion. What do you think?"

Inez leaned forward in the saddle, pressing the stallion down from his half rear, then nodded her agreement and continued riding Bayfire just as she would any other horse who'd done something unexpected.

Only once, when he crowded Witch and got kicked, did Inez slip and call the stallion by name.

"He knows better than that," Inez said, petting the stallion's shoulder and leaning forward to check for scratches or wounds.

"So does she," Jake said, in a voice so tight that Sam looked over to see why.

Jake was blushing. His mahogany skin turned darker and his jaw was set. He must have been distracted, too.

"They've all worked pretty hard," Inez said. "Maybe it's time to head toward those hot springs."

"Good idea," Sam said.

She didn't check with Jake, because she could see he'd already started his version of scolding Witch. He backed her, turned her, and backed again, reminding her he was the rider and she was the obedient horse.

Ace tightened beneath Sam. She felt his muscles tense as he looked at a level, open stretch of range.

"You've been a good boy all morning," she said to him. "Wanna run?" Ace jerked his muzzle high and snorted. "I'm going to let him out here," Sam told Inez, so that she wouldn't be surprised if Bayfire tried to follow.

And then she did.

The little gelding swept into a gallop, and Sam

heard hooves behind her, but Bayfire wasn't catching them. When Sam risked a quick glance back, she saw the stallion's gallop was more picturesque than swift, as if he heard theme music in his head, accompanying each reach and recoil of his fine legs.

When Inez and Sam finally rested the horses by stripping off their saddles and riding them bareback into the hot springs on Mrs. Allen's ranch, Jake stayed astride Witch, away from the edge.

"Are you punishing her?" Sam asked.

Jake shook his head. "No, just in case something changes, one of us should be mounted up."

Sam wasn't sure that made sense, until Bayfire blew through his lips while watching Witch. Was he trying to get her attention?

If so, it probably wasn't working the way he wanted it to, Sam thought. The mare flattened her ears and feinted a bite his way.

"Does she like anyone?" Inez asked quietly.

"She likes Jake," Sam said, swishing her bare feet in the water around Ace.

"Mostly," Jake said.

Inez laughed, then threw one leg over her horse's neck and slipped off into the water beside him. With only a small splash, she let her head go under the warm water.

"This is heaven," Inez said as she emerged, hair and clothing soaked, face beaded with water. "The bottom is kind of slimy," she admitted, shivering as if her toes were gripping something unpleasant, "but do you know what you'd pay for a horse and rider spa in Los Angeles?"

"I have no idea," Sam said, wondering if there really was such a thing.

"Me either, but I know it wouldn't be free!" Inez was still laughing when Bayfire joined in the fun.

Tossing his black forelock away from his eyes, the stallion backed a few splashing steps before giving Inez a hard nudge between the shoulder blades. The push knocked Inez, face first, beneath the surface again.

Coughing and clutching her hat, Inez reemerged with a suspicious look.

"He's playing," Sam said quickly. Remembering Inez's bruised shoulder, she couldn't blame the trainer for being cautious.

Relieved, Inez played back, scooting her palm along the water's surface to splash the stallion.

Bayfire lowered his lips and swept his head back and forth, until he'd stirred a froth of bubbles.

It might be one of his tricks. The nudge might have been, too, but he'd decided to use them for fun.

This had to be progress, Sam thought. Carefully, she rode Ace out of the slippery sided pool.

She met Jake's eyes and she must have looked expectant, because he gave a slight nod.

"He's loosening up a little," Sam said. "It really hasn't been that hard to get him to do it."

"Almost too easy," Jake said.

Even though Ace picked that moment to shake like a big brown dog, splattering Jake and Witch with water, Jake looked as satisfied with their day's work as Sam felt.

The three riders' haze of satisfaction spiked as they approached the bridge leading to River Bend Ranch and caught the aroma of barbecue smoke.

"Oh, that smells incredible," Inez moaned. "Tie me up and gag me if I ever again suggest opening a can of soup in my camper instead of eating your grandmother's cooking."

"Sure," Sam said.

Feeling their riders' elation, all three horses had broken into playful trots when they spotted something purple and realized Violette Lee had returned and stood near the hitching rail, talking to Pepper.

She must not have come by plane, this time, Sam thought, but the thought floated away like dust when Sam saw that the young cowboy, named for his chili-pepper-red hair, was enchanted by the actress.

No wonder, Sam thought.

Today, Violette looked more like a movie star. She still wore ratty jeans and her hair looked no cleaner than it had before, but her silky lavender blouse was pretty, even if it fit as if she'd last worn it as a child actress on that Santa Claus show.

Despite her tight blouse, Violette looked truly interested in whatever Pepper was saying, Sam realized. Sam tried to shake off her critical attitude, but it was too late. Violette had sensed the disapproval of all three riders, and it was like pouring gasoline on a fire. Her tone turned chirpy and she rested her small hand on Pepper's arm.

Sam had no idea what the two had been talking about, but as Sam was dismounting in front of the hitching rail, she glimpsed Pepper's expression. He was flattered despite his discomfort.

"Oh, ma'am," he said to Violette, "I'm all dirty from haying. You don't want to come anywhere close to me."

"Don't be silly," Violette said.

Jake had stopped Witch across the ranch yard, close to the ten-acre pasture, but Inez rode right up beside Sam.

"Did you hear that?" Sam demanded in an outraged whisper.

"I hope you don't expect me to do anything," Inez answered. "I can't call her off like a trained animal, unfortunately."

Sam's brain ticked off all the advice Brynna had given her about working with the HARP girls, remembering that bad behavior should be ignored because any kind of attention was good attention, to some people.

So Sam really tried to ignore Violette. It wasn't

like she was jealous, but it was embarrassing to watch Pepper fall all over himself simply because the actress was talking to him.

Swallowing back her irritation, and remarks that would have sounded dumb anyway, Sam was just closing the gate to the ten-acre pasture behind Ace when Violette left Pepper to trail after Inez and Bayfire.

Pepper hurried up beside Sam.

"That's Violette Lee," Pepper gasped.

"I know," Sam said.

She tried to sound impressed. After all, only yesterday she'd marveled at the actress walking out of Gram's kitchen. And Sam couldn't wait to tell Jen. She would have already if this entire movie thing hadn't been declared top secret. And if the telephone wasn't in the middle of the kitchen where everyone would overhear her breaking her promise to protect Inez's privacy.

"She was talking to me," Pepper said. "Did you see?"

"I did," Sam said, and Pepper didn't notice her lack of enthusiasm. He was still floating.

"I can't believe it," Pepper said. "I think I'll call home and tell the folks."

Sam didn't bother telling him the whole movie was secret. Pepper had run away from his home in Idaho several years ago and Sam had never heard him talk about his family. It was kind of cool that he wanted to call home, and it wasn't like his parents were going to leave Idaho for Nevada, just to see Violette Lee.

Shaking his head, Pepper stared down at his forearm. His cuff was turned back and hay stuck to his sweaty skin. There was nothing worth staring at except that it was probably the arm Violette had touched.

"She's even more beautiful than in the movies," he said.

Boy, he did have stars in his eyes, Sam thought, as she watched him set his boots meandering in the direction of the bunkhouse.

Then she saw Jake. He'd left Witch ground-tied, and maybe because he'd told her off about Violette before, she assumed he was going to do it again.

He was walking toward her, pointing. At what? Starstruck Pepper?

Sam almost growled. If Jake tried to give her one more bit of advice, he was in big trouble.

"I'm not listening to anything you—" Sam broke off as the pasture gate slammed against her back.

The impact of wood didn't hurt, but she knew at once why Jake had been pointing, and it had nothing to do with Violette or Pepper.

Because she'd been distracted, she hadn't closed the gate bolt completely.

Ace had used his nimble lips to open it, and he was shouldering through the open gate, returning to the ranch yard.

"What a clever animal," Violette called from where she stood beside Inez. "Did you teach him to do that?"

It was more important to stop her horse than answer, so Sam shouted, "Ace!"

She knew the horse was too weary to go anyplace. He nudged the gate every single time she locked him up. It was a habit and this time he'd caught her being careless. Thank goodness Dad had already gone into the house.

"You, there!" Violette called.

"That's Samantha," Inez reminded the actress.

Because there was no mistaking the edge of irritation in the trainer's voice, Sam smiled at her. Violette didn't seem to notice Inez's tone or Sam's smile.

"I asked," Violette said with false patience, "if you taught him that—oh, how precious."

Ace came to Sam and hung his head over her shoulder.

"You are precious, aren't you," Sam said, kissing his nose. "And you think I'm such a sucker for your hugs that I'll forgive you."

Of course, she did.

Sam started to walk the gelding back to the ten-acre pasture, but Violette called out, "Please don't take him away yet."

Sam stopped, and Ace whirled with wide eyes,

nostrils, and pricked ears, to face Violette.

Startled, Sam had nearly decided the actress had an uncanny knack with animals, when Violette reached in her pocket and pulled out two sugar cubes.

"Go ahead," Sam told Ace, when he gave a low whinny and stepped away from her and toward Violette.

As if I had a choice, Sam thought, as Violette fed the horse and spoke to him in baby talk.

"He's a smart, smart boy, isn't him?" Violette cooed as Ace licked her palm, looking for more sugar.

Then Jake's low laugh, entirely too close and too amused, made her look at him.

He held both palms toward her, as if fending off an attack.

"One more itty, bitty sugar cube won't hurt, and he'll go right back in that icky old pasture where him belongs, won't he?" Violette coaxed Ace back to the pasture and bolted the gate behind him.

This time he didn't test it, of course, and Violette looked totally pleased with herself as she walked back over to Inez.

Sam double-checked the bolt, watching as Ace trotted lazily across the dry grass. Was he on his way to share his joke with the other horses?

Jake stood with folded arms. For a second, he watched Ace, too, but then his head turned her way.

"Don't say anything," Sam told him, and then Violette started saying things to Inez that even

Jake couldn't ignore.

She was talking about Ace.

"With some creative camera work, he could be Bay's double," the actress insisted. "Don't you think? After all, the script calls for my character"—Violette beckoned for Sam and Jake to come closer—"which at that point is the princess pretending to be the pauper . . ." She tossed her lank hair without disturbing her sunglasses.

"It's all very Elizabethan, since they're twins, separated at birth. I play both roles. At any rate, the script calls for me to steal a horse off the street. It's supposed to be a scrubby little thing, which is rather a stretch for Bayfire, but he was to be muddied up a bit, right?" she asked Inez, then rushed on. "So your little horse would be perfect for closeups. They're going after this whole 'grit and determination are more important than bloodlines' kind of theme, you know?"

Sam thought it sounded like a good idea for a movie, but she didn't like what Violette was implying about Ace.

"It's an underdog movie," Violette emphasized, as if they hadn't understood her before. "I tell you he'd be perfect. Although . . . ," Violette paused. As she stared at Ace in the pasture, her manicured fingers plucked at the air as if she were touching the gelding's mane. "He could use some hair extensions."

Hair extensions? Her mustang cow pony would

never wear hair extensions.

Sam swallowed hard.

"I don't think so," she said calmly, and Inez saw the frustration in Sam's eyes, even if Jake didn't.

"Sam, could you please do me a favor?" Inez asked.

Violette's forehead creased, as if she couldn't imagine why Inez was being so polite, as Sam nodded.

"I'd be so grateful," Inez continued, "if you could check and see if the box stall is open to the corral. That way Bayfire can just put himself to bed when he's ready."

"Sure," Sam said. "I need to check on Tempest and Sunny, anyway."

When she got there, of course the stall was already open to the pasture.

She let out a long, relieved breath, then leaned against the barn wall with her eyes closed.

A tiny neigh made Sam's eyes open. Tempest's nostrils flared wide open as she angled her head through the wooden slats of her stall.

"Of course I'll pet you, baby," Sam said.

Her back was to the barn door and she was kneading the filly's silky ears when she heard Jake's footsteps.

"What would I have to do," Sam asked, "to get you to shut up and go away?"

Chapter Twelve ๛

"Can't think of anything that'd make me go now," Jake said, then took a deep breath. "Hurricane, maybe."

"Get it over with, then," Sam said. She could hear her own long-suffering tone. "Give me another of your stupid lectures."

"She's not a real princess."

"Duh," Sam said, then crossed her arms.

She stared past Jake and saw Gram talking to Violette, probably begging her to stay for dinner.

"She's not a redcoat general's daughter," Jake said, jerking his head in Violette's direction. "Or Annie Oakley, either."

"I know that, Jake. She's an actress."

"Someone needs to tell her so," Jake said, "and it might as well be you."

Sam gave up the idea of telling Jake, again, that such a thing would be rude. Why couldn't he see that?

Maybe Violette would be less unpleasant after she'd settled in—except that wouldn't happen. Inez had said time was tight. The crew only had a few days here.

And Jake *was* basically a polite guy. He must think that this was a desperate situation.

"Why don't you tell her?" Sam asked.

"It wouldn't be right," Jake said with certainty.

A legend crossed Sam's mind. Something about a great hero who'd lost his strength when his magic hair was snipped off. She weighed the consequences of relating that story to Jake.

Bad idea, she thought. If she wanted to keep Jake as a friend, she wouldn't tell him he was a chicken.

"She's rich and famous, but she's also this thin little scrap of a female," Jake said. "I'd look like a bully."

Jake had a point.

"I'll think about it," Sam said, then glanced out into the ranch yard, where Violette and Inez stood near the house. "But I'm not doing it at dinner."

"'Course not," Jake said. "To tell you the truth, she's kinda scary."

"Scary," Sam repeated, looking at Jake, who'd

never shown a speck of cowardice, at least in front of her. "What about her could possibly be scary?"

"All that sweetie, baby, horsy stuff is weird."

Sam giggled, then socked Jake in the arm. "I'll take care of her for you, partner," Sam said. "Don't you worry."

He nodded solemnly and headed for the barn door. He was almost through, and Sam had started to relax, when Jake looked back, made a cowboy gun of his hand, and said, "Don't take too long about it. I'm leavin' soon and this is one showdown I don't want to miss."

"What I can't understand," Violette was saying as she and Inez walked toward the house in answer to Gram's summons, "is why this horseback jump is done in the wrong costume. Tell the truth, Inez, wouldn't it have more visual impact if I were wearing a medieval gown rather than the clothes of a peasant?"

"*You* won't be wearing either one in that scene," Inez reminded her.

Violette gave an indulgent smile. Then, amazingly, she held the door so Inez could enter the kitchen first.

"So you say."

At least that's what Sam thought Violette muttered, but she didn't spend even a minute worrying about it. The aroma of grilled steak reminded her she'd eaten next to nothing all day.

Seconds later, she almost stepped on Violette Lee.

The actress knelt in the middle of the kitchen floor. She petted Blaze with one hand and stroked Cougar with the other, while the cat rubbed against her.

When Violette looked up, her lips curved in a genuine smile. She'd taken off her sunglasses, too, and her eyes were an amazing shade of lavender.

"Your pets are wonderful," Violette said. Then she noticed Dad and Brynna hovered, not sitting at their places at the table. "But I'm delaying dinner."

She gave Blaze a kiss on the top of the head, managed to touch the tip of Cougar's tail as he slipped away, then stood.

She gave her hands a quick swipe against her jeans as she approached the table. Sam noticed Gram's grimace. Gram wanted to remind Violette to wash her hands before eating, but she didn't.

Sam found herself seated at the far end of the table, facing Gram at the head of it. Inez and Violette sat together, across from Dad, Brynna, and Jake, who squeezed in next to them.

"Thanks so much, again, for inviting us," Inez said.

"Well, I just hope it's as good as you're used to," Gram said as she approached with two filled plates for the guests.

Sam had glimpsed Gram's preparations on the

counter and stove as she came in. Steak and baked potatoes and sautéed vegetables—good ones, this time—were arranged on the plates. Spinach salads already sat at everyone's places.

"Oh!" Violette looked suddenly sick. She recoiled from the plate, then struggled to cover her revulsion. "I didn't mention being a vegetarian, because I didn't want you to go to any extra trouble, but I'm afraid I can't eat that beef."

"I see," Gram replied. Taking the change in stride, she handed one plate to Inez and the other to Brynna.

Sam could see Jake scoffing, but she thought it was kind of cool. Lots of people claimed to love animals, but had no problem eating them. Violette might be a self-centered brat, but she was a brat with principles.

"I just hope you'll have enough," Gram said, arranging a plate with extra vegetables in place of the steak. "I don't have tofu or anything like that."

"Tofu's overrated," Violette said, rolling her eyes. "And this will be fine." Violette accepted the plate, and her attitude wasn't snobbish at all.

When everyone had begun eating, Brynna asked Inez if she didn't find it difficult working with zebras.

"I've heard they don't shake off their wildness like wild horses," Brynna said.

"They're a challenge, but they're part of what Animal Artists has always been, and—" Inez broke off, looking distracted for a minute. "Actually, I have no serious problems working with equines—zebras, mules, horses, or donkeys. It's communication with the directors and actors that's more difficult."

"Very funny," Violette said as she picked a small piece of bacon out of her spinach salad.

"Not you," Inez said. "I'm thinking more of non-horse people. They have to be taught what a horse can and can't do. You can only shoot so many takes before the horse gets tired or bored or realizes he doesn't like the rubber shoes on his hooves that keep him from slipping."

"Wyatt, do you want to put Blaze out?" Gram asked as the Border collie stood panting next to Violette. "He's being a nuisance."

"Don't!" Violette told Dad. "I mean, please don't. I love animals. And he's just waiting for more bacon. It's my fault for feeding him at the table."

"Guess it won't turn into a habit just this one time," Dad said.

As he settled back into his chair, Sam saw her own amazement mirrored on Jake's face. Neither of them could believe Dad was allowing this.

"Didn't you have pets growing up?" Gram asked gently.

Inez made a determined cut into her steak and her expression said she knew what would follow, but Sam was eager to hear about Violette's childhood. It couldn't have been an ordinary one.

"No, I lived with my mother until pretty recently,"

Violette said. "I've always loved animals, but she had no use for them. I remember luring stray cats to our deck in Malibu." Sam noticed everyone's smiles slip when Violette added, "Until my mother threw scalding water on them."

"Why?" Sam cried out.

Violette fidgeted with the sunglasses she'd placed next to her plate. For a second, Sam thought she was about to put them on, but she didn't.

"She said they took up time I could be using to become a better actress," Violette explained. "She said they were dirty, too, getting paw prints on the hardwood floors. And they must have, because she always knew when I'd sneaked one inside. The time she found cat hair on her black cashmere sweater—" Violette stopped.

For an instant, she covered her lips with both hands, shook her head in denial, as if her offense had just been discovered. Then, finally, she went on.

"She wouldn't let me go to bed until I'd examined every black garment in her closet and picked off the hairs with tweezers."

Brynna looked shocked. One of her hands dropped beneath the table. Sam just knew she was touching the bulge of her baby.

Dad looked angry.

Except for the swing of the grandfather clock's pendulum in the other room, there was silence.

Isn't that child abuse? Sam wondered.

But it was long over and Brynna's sympathy broke the accusing hush.

"Your mother sounds like a very particular woman."

Violette gave a humorless laugh. "You could say that, but I had the animals of the Claus show, and their trainers were so nice to me, you wouldn't believe it."

"You were the baby of the cast," Inez reminded her.

"Yeah, and the work was such a . . ." Violette pressed the heels of both hands against her temples. "I don't know, an onslaught on my brain, that most afternoons all I wanted was to curl up beside the reindeer, in all that scratchy straw, and pillow my head against them. Their coats are so thick. . . ." Violette's voice trailed off and her face wore a dreamy, little-girl look.

Inez's hands were jerky as she sipped her milk. She kept her eyes on Violette as if she was worried about what the actress would say next. Then, before Violette went on, she nudged her with a question.

"Tell everyone about reindeer hair. What's so special about it? I always forget," Inez said.

"Oh, well, it's like no other on earth," Violette began, and then she launched into an almost scientific description of specially evolved hair that protected the huge deer against subzero temperatures.

Inez sighed, seeming relieved, before Violette

interrupted her own explanation to say, "I was such a little kid while I was starring in that show, that when the reindeer's trainer lifted off their harnesses at the end of the day, I wanted to take off my clothes, too."

"That's natural enough," Gram said, chuckling, but Sam saw Gram's sideways glance meet Brynna's.

"I don't know if it is or not," Violette said, "I just know that one day, when I actually started to do it, my mother yanked my red velvet shirt down over my tummy. Then I had to go and say something like, 'My harness never gets lifted off.' Everyone thought that was way profound, but my mother was humiliated." Violette turned to Inez, as if she were about to give her a cue. "Mom thought I made her sound like the world's worst stage mother."

"Which of course she was," Inez said, before touching her napkin to her lips and leaning across the table toward Jake, who'd kept quiet all this time. "Jake, remind me what we're doing tomorrow with Bayfire."

"Lost Canyon," Jake said.

"Yes . . . ," Inez said, probing for more details, but Jake looked reluctant.

He took a quick glance at Violette as if he didn't want her to hear what he had to say next. At first Sam was irritated. Didn't Jake have any compassion? But then Sam remembered why he was hesitant to talk about Lost Canyon in front of Violette.

"We're checking out the site for the waterfall

jump, remember?" Jake said.

"Oh yeah," Inez said, then made a joke of her mistake by gently hitting her hand against her head.

"I can hardly wait!" Violette said. "That will be so exciting!"

"Vi," Inez said, cautioning her. "You're not riding in this scene."

All the little-girl giddiness dropped from Violette's face and tone and she grabbed her sunglasses from their place beside her unused knife.

As soon as she slipped them on, she was once more the sly and elegant actress.

"Of course not, darling," she told Inez. "When I'm not wanted, you only have to tell me once."

Chapter Thirteen ❧

*A*fter dinner, Inez drove Violette through Alkali and back to Darton, where she was staying in a small hotel. Although Sam thought Inez was nice to offer, it caused another coldly worded argument, because Violette wanted to spend the night in Inez's camper.

Inez had protested that there simply wasn't room, and instead of offering her a bed for the night, as Sam expected, Brynna and Dad had seemed oddly eager to clear and wash the dishes and stay out of the conversation completely.

Jake was gone, too, and Sam had walked halfway to the barn to check on Tempest, when she realized Gram was right behind her.

"Wait for me, honey," Gram said, but she

lengthened her strides so that Sam barely needed to pause.

Walking through the twilight without her apron or garden hat, Gram looked young. Sam felt a tug of amazement, realizing Gram had actually been pregnant with Dad, years ago, just as Brynna was pregnant with the new baby now.

For some reason, it was just hard to believe.

Before they reached the barn, Sweetheart nickered from the ten-acre pasture, greeting Gram.

"I'll be back in a minute, old girl," Gram called to her.

Guilt nudged Sam as she realized Gram was the only one who regularly gave the mare attention. Sure, they used her once in a while with the most cautious HARP girls, but she didn't get the daily pats and hugs Ace and Tempest did.

"You should watch me halter Tempest," Sam said proudly as Gram walked beside her into the barn. "She's doing so well."

"I will later," Gram said before Sam could lift the halter from its hook. "But there's something we need to talk about."

"Okay," Sam said carefully.

"I've already asked your father, and he's down-right enthusiastic. He thinks it's the best thing, but I—" Gram broke off and smiled softly as she held both Sam's shoulders in her hands. "Honey, this time it's me asking for your permission to do something."

Chills rained down Sam's neck and arms. Dozens of possibilities should be leaping across her mind, but she thought of nothing. She only knew this couldn't be anything good. Gram looked too serious.

"With your permission," Gram repeated the word again, "Sweetheart and I will be joining the riding therapy program together."

"Okay," Sam said again, feeling confused.

"That means she'll live in their stable all the time. River Bend Ranch will be donating her to the program, so that even on days I'm not there, the children can use her." Though the barn was warm from the day's August heat, Sam froze.

"You're giving away Mom's horse," Sam said, finally understanding.

Gram sighed and nodded.

Suddenly Sam remembered a photograph Dad had shown her of Mom in her wedding dress, riding the spirited young pinto, Sweetheart. Mom's smile had been radiant as Sweetheart pranced. But that day had been long ago.

"She's a good horse," Sam protested.

"Honey, she's a wonderful horse. Sweetheart has love and experience to give, but no one asks anything of her."

"But she's happy out in the pasture," Sam said.

"She's bored, Samantha. She's getting fat and losing muscle. She's left out of all the excitement around here, and I think she knows it." Gram paused, giving Sam a lopsided smile. "Don't think I'm talking about myself, either. I can go to New Mexico for cooking classes or do things down at the church, but Sweetheart's stuck."

Sam refused to cry. She looked up into the barn rafters. Last Christmas she'd felt as if Mom's angel hovered up there, watching over her. What would Mom want her to do now?

As if the words had been whispered in her ear, Sam said, "In that program, Sweetheart would be at the center of everything, instead of on the fringes."

"That's right," Gram said. "And don't you know those children would just love her to death?"

Sam nodded. Sweetheart would have a second life, surrounded by affectionate children who'd touch that heart-shaped spot on her side a hundred times a week and tell her she was beautiful.

The guilt Sam had felt as they passed the mare just minutes ago came back. "I'll give her more attention. I promise. Sunny and Tempest and Ace can do with a little less. I spoil them anyway."

"Honey, you're just one person and school's starting," Gram said. "None of us has the time to make her as happy as she could be there."

"Okay, I'll do it. I mean, it's okay if you do it. You have my permission," Sam said in a rush. "But I'm going out to the pasture with her right now!"

Sam left Gram standing in the barn.

Running as fast as she could, Sam headed for the

part of the pasture where Sweetheart's white spots stood out in the dusk. Then Sam climbed the fence.

The old mare tossed her head up in surprise, but she didn't back off even a step.

She's so gentle, Sam thought. Kids with crutches wouldn't spook her. Kids who were awkward mounting or too enthusiastic to play with smaller animals wouldn't faze Sweetheart at all.

Sam threw her arms around the warm pinto neck, pressed her face into it, and then she did cry.

"I don't want to let you go!" she told the horse. "I love you, Sweetheart. I haven't shown it as much as I should have and I'm sorry. I know you'll be happier with those little kids, and I'm so sorry."

The old mare shook her head and then she did back a step, but Sam could tell Sweetheart wasn't escaping her hug. Sweetheart was trying to get a better look at Sam and figure out what was wrong.

"Why do things have to change?" she asked the horse.

The old mare blew through her lips and shook her mane, but no matter how long Sam waited—and the grass was wet with dew by the time she said good-bye—neither of them came up with an answer.

Brynna woke Sam at dawn.

Sam's face felt stiff and her eyelids were swollen from crying, but she didn't feel a bit groggy.

"What?" Sam said, struggling to sit up and open

her eyes, the instant Brynna jiggled her arm.

"Inez wants to head out for Lost Canyon right now."

"How come?" Sam asked, pushing her hair back from her face.

"Two reasons. First, because the director of her camera crew says the weather forecast for tomorrow includes early morning fog, perfect for this scene, which is supposed to be taking place in England and—are you awake enough for all this, Sam?"

"Yeah," Sam said.

As if he were testing her, Cougar eased away from his place on her quilt and slipped by Sam, set on burrowing into her warm sheets. When Sam caught him and tried to pull him onto her lap, Cougar leaped for the floor and Brynna continued.

"The other thing is, Inez thinks Violette might come back, and she doesn't want her to follow you out there."

"Okay," Sam said.

She swung her legs out of bed and snatched her jeans and a shirt from the floor.

"A truly wicked stepmother would point out the uses of hangers and chests of drawers," Brynna joked.

"Sorry," Sam said, voice muffled as she pulled the yellow tee-shirt over her head.

"Who cares?" Brynna said, and Sam emerged smiling.

"I guess you're not so wicked," Sam told her, then asked, "Is Jake here?"

"Not yet," Brynna said, watching Sam look for a sock to match the one she held. "But I called. Maxine told me he's already left Three Ponies. So, as soon as he gets here, I'll send him riding after you and Inez."

"Good," Sam said. Then she noticed Brynna's frown.

"I don't think there'll be anything on this ride that you can't handle yourself," Brynna said. "Do you?"

"No," Sam said, puzzled. "Oh, why did I say 'good'? Is that what you're asking?"

When Brynna nodded and leaned patiently against the doorframe, Sam's words came tumbling out before she meant them to.

"It's just that Jake and I haven't been getting along that well. He thinks I'm being too nice to Violette," Sam confessed.

"I knew something was going on," Brynna said. "Swear you won't breathe a word of this to him, and I'll tell you what Maxine said."

Sam made a little-kid motion of crossing her heart, then held up her hand.

"I promise," she said, still searching for the other sock, this time under her bed.

"He's worried that he's been too protective of you, and that you won't know what to do without him to stand up for you."

"What? How could she possibly know that?" Sam

asked, astounded. She couldn't imagine Jake telling anyone such a thing. Especially his mother.

"Let's see if I've got this right," Brynna said, tilting her head to one side. "He told something like that to Nate and Nate told . . ." Brynna grimaced, afraid she'd get it wrong. "Quinn? Or maybe I have that backward. Maybe Jake told Quinn and he told Nate? Anyway, one of the boys told their dad."

"And he told Jake's mom," Sam concluded. She shook her head at the disloyalty of brothers. "I'm kind of glad not to have any siblings." Without meaning to, her eyes dropped to Brynna's middle. "Yet."

Brynna rubbed the bulge of the baby. "This little one won't be telling your secrets for a while."

A quiet hummed between them as Sam finally found her other sock. The silence wasn't awkward. It was actually kind of cozy, and Sam realized she was really starting to be excited about her new brother or sister.

"If I was really sappy," Sam muttered to herself, "I'd tell myself some changes are good."

"I don't know exactly what you mean," Brynna said, yawning. "But if you're talking about buying some new socks, I'm all for it."

The previous day's hard work had only made Ace and Bayfire more spirited. Inez and Sam started out playing follow-the-leader and ended up in a game of anything-you-can-do-I-can-do-better.

Inez still didn't talk to Bayfire, pretending this was just ordinary riding, as the day before had been, but she was really preparing Bayfire for the next day's stunts.

"The crew's already been out here and installed the rubber mats for the jump," Inez told Sam.

"Rubber mats?" Sam asked.

"Textured rubber floor mats," Inez explained. "Since we're working on public land, we got permission from BLM to install them as long as we pull them up when we're done. They'll give Bayfire's hooves better traction on takeoff and landing."

"Good idea," Sam said, thinking how slick the rocks in Lost Canyon could be, especially if it was a foggy morning.

Inez shrugged. "We take all kinds of safety precautions for the animals. When Bayfire worked in _Little Sure Shot_, we had to pack his ears with cotton to protect him from the incessant—though pretend—gunfire."

"What if something still goes wrong?" Sam asked. She didn't mention Violette, but that's who she was thinking about.

"We'll have a vet on scene. You know him, in fact," Inez said.

"Dr. Scott?" Sam asked.

"That's the one," Inez told her. "Apparently the makeup crew was practicing wounds on a horse pastured near Clara's and he was startled by their realism.

But he'll be up here, and we have sort of an ambulance trailer, too, just in case. And most important of all, we'll have a bucket of grain. Nothing settles a guy's nerves like a snack," she said, rubbing the stallion's withers.

They looked for shale hillsides to climb and descend. When they spotted a willow tree alongside the river with drooping branches, they rode beneath them.

Sam was giggling from the long tickling willows, when they emerged and Inez said, "Speaking of 'just in case . . .'"

"Were we?" Sam asked, wondering what Inez was talking about.

"Yeah," Inez said. When she pulled down the bill of her green cap just the way Jake did with his Stetson, Sam wondered what Inez was up to. "Remember, I said we had the ambulance standing by just in case."

"Oh, right," Sam said.

"Well, I want you to be my backup," Inez blurted. "Just in case Bayfire isn't up to the jump tomorrow, I'd like you to do it with Ace."

Sam's head spun. She actually felt dizzy at the idea of jumping from rock to rock on the rim of Lost Canyon.

"I can't," she said.

"Well, let's wait and take a look at it," Inez offered.

"I've taken a look at it," Sam said, "and even with those traction mats, I'd be too scared."

Inez's gaze lowered to Ace. She wet her lips.

"I'd be too scared for me *and* Ace," Sam added.

Inez shrugged. "It was just an idea. After Violette brought it up yesterday, I couldn't get it out of my head." Inez sighed. "Don't give it another thought, okay? But I would like to put Bayfire over a few jumps today, just to get him geared up for the big one."

As they approached Lost Canyon, Sam remembered a gulch.

"Don't know if you want to try it," she told Inez, "but there's a gully left from the time the river flooded. It's a little too wide to jump and a little too narrow to comfortably ride down one side and up the other."

"Is that a dare?" Inez asked, and then, as if he understood, Bayfire gathered himself.

Inez smiled and raised her eyebrows, though she didn't say a word to the horse.

"Which are you going to do?" Inez asked.

"Go around it," Sam said. "I know Ace can do it. He has before, but there's no reason to take a chance."

Inez looked undecided, so Sam pointed out the path she'd take.

"How about here?" Sam said, guiding Ace up a sloping trail.

Inez nodded, sending Bayfire up the hard way. Her black ponytail bounced as the horse lunged upward, threading between boulders, until they reached a narrow ledge.

When the trail led back down and there were no real obstacles, Inez switched directions, heading back toward the gully.

"Here we go," Sam told Ace as Bayfire moved into a gallop, jumping wide clumps of sagebrush as he went.

At first, Ace veered around the gray-green vegetation, but once he understood Sam was asking for senseless jackrabbit hops, he set out after the stallion, popping over the sagebrush with ease.

When they reached the gully, the horses took it side by side, and landed with less elation than their riders.

"Good boy," Sam told Ace, and when she leaned down to give him a hearty pat on the neck, he snorted, wondering what all the fuss was about.

Resting her horse as they moved into Lost Canyon, Sam let him fall behind. She chalked up his careful, deliberate walk to being out of breath, until Ace snorted and stood stone still.

Bayfire and Inez went on ahead. The stallion's head jerked from right to left as he inspected the unfamiliar surroundings.

Sam tightened her legs a little, then clucked to Ace.

"They're getting ahead of us, boy. Let's pick up the pace just a little," Sam urged the gelding.

When Ace still refused, Sam looked for trouble. She thought of the cougar, of Flick, the mustanger, who'd actually threatened Jake with a rifle, but she didn't see any danger.

"What are you thinking, Ace?" Sam said, rubbing Ace's neck.

Inez drew rein, waiting for them to catch up.

"I have to say Bay has better nerves than I do," Inez observed. "It's a little creepy for me, working this near the edge," Inez said, looking down at the adobe and honey-colored layers of sandstone below. "But he doesn't seem to mind it."

"I'm looking for the path up," Sam said. She stared at the soaring rock, glad she'd refused to help with the stunt. "It should be here, since we're almost to the 'waterfall.' I just never took it before."

As Inez urged Bayfire back toward the middle of the narrow trail, Ace took a few slow steps to follow.

Sam was leaning, looking around for the trail to the top, and not quite balanced in her saddle when she saw Inez point.

"Is that a wild horse?" Inez gasped.

A roan filly and two blood bays scattered off the trail ahead, away from the big boulder with water seeping down its face.

"Oh yeah," Sam answered in a whisper. "They're wild."

The words had barely passed her lips before the three mustangs vanished and the Phantom appeared. Ace must have scented him minutes ago.

"I don't even believe it. That's the stallion, the leader!" Inez's voice was low and excited.

Sam felt as if her nerve endings were every bit as alive and vibrating as the horses'.

Morning sunlight glimmered on the Phantom's coat, turning it silvery white. His head lifted and his brown eyes peered through wavy strands of forelock that crowned him king of this canyon.

"He's magnificent," Inez said. "And he's not afraid. He's watching us."

He's watching Bayfire, Sam thought. Her hands gripped the reins hard. She told herself everything was okay. So far.

Eyes wide and nostrils flared, the Phantom took in all he needed to know about the other stallion. With his herd safely out of sight, he didn't challenge Bayfire.

But the tame stallion clearly felt threatened. Sam's heart went out to Bayfire as he mouthed his bit and lowered his head.

Was Inez ashamed or just impatient with Bayfire? Whatever the reason, she tried to make him stand still and the dark stallion panicked. Squealing, Bayfire backed swiftly toward the edge of the trail.

Seeing his possible opponent retreat, the Phantom snorted and turned to follow his herd.

Don't go, Sam thought, *not so soon.*

But it was for the best, because Inez was struggling with Bayfire as he kept moving off the trail, toward the dangerous, sandy edge.

"Stand," Inez ordered, but Bayfire didn't.

He stopped for just an instant, and then, seeing the silken swaying of the Phantom's tail as he moved off in easy victory, Bayfire screamed a defiant neigh.

"Are you crazy?" Inez asked.

Beneath her, Sam felt Ace shiver. He gave a worried whinny and sidestepped away from Bayfire.

Sam didn't blame the little gelding. He didn't want to be anyplace near the two stallions if a fight erupted.

But the Phantom wasn't fooled. He knew Bayfire was no battle-hardened rival. The silver stallion strutted off without a backward look.

Blowing and huffing, Bayfire let every creature around know he felt insulted. His trumpeting neigh blurred Inez's words.

"Let's go," she said, but was the trainer talking to her horse?

Sam studied Inez's face, but she only saw concentration. Completely focused, she used hands, legs, and seat to give the stallion orders any saddle horse would be able to follow. He ignored her.

Finally, Inez tapped his withers with her hand. She spoke low commands and though his ears flicked back to catch her words, he struck out with one hind hoof. He slung his head side to side, trying to capture the bit, until he heard hooves, moving up the trail behind him.

He swung around to face the approaching horse and in that moment, Sam saw the bay stallion as he should be. Defiant and strong, barely restricted by his rider, he was dangerous and definitely not a horse she'd want to be riding, but beautiful.

"Jake's coming," Sam said as she recognized Witch's bad-tempered snort.

"Maybe Witch'll make him forget about that stallion," Inez muttered, arms shaking with the effort of holding the horse. "I can't believe this. He's totally out of control."

It took Jake to realize what neither Sam nor Inez did.

He drew Witch to a halt, bumped his Stetson back from his eyes. In amazement, he looked from Sam to Inez, then back to Sam.

"What did you do to that horse?" he asked her. "Whatever it was, keep it up. Looks to me like he's cured."

Chapter Fourteen ❧

$\mathcal{I}$t took fifteen minutes to get Bayfire settled down enough that he was willing to stand near Witch and Ace as they drank from the small pool at the base of the rock face.

Sam and Jake had dismounted, but Inez remained in the saddle, certain she had better control of the stallion from there.

"Obviously, in spite of the fact that he's recovered some of his spirit, I'm not going to chase after a wild stallion and get us both killed," Inez said.

"Look at him strut," Sam said, laughing.

Neck bowed to his chest, nostrils flared and red as if he'd run up the mountain and back again, Bayfire bared his teeth toward the empty trail where the Phantom had stood, then half reared, forelegs pawing in battle with a horse that wasn't there.

"I'm not joking, you two," Inez said. "He's hardly under control and he hasn't even seen the site where we'll be shooting tomorrow."

"Kinda wondered why you went on past the trail to the top," Jake said.

"We missed it," Sam said, suppressing a shiver. "I've never been up there before."

"It's no big deal," Jake said, looking at Sam as if she'd said she was terrified.

"I didn't say it was," Sam snapped. "Just because I've never gone up there before doesn't mean I'm afraid."

"Good," Inez said, "because I'd feel safer if you two rode alongside us, kind of sandwiching Bayfire between your horses. That is, if there's room?" She looked at Jake.

"Just barely," he said.

Oh good, Sam thought, as she swung Ace into position beside the snorting stallion, but it wasn't as bad as she thought.

The trail was on the windward side of the canyon, but the summer day was calm and the only hazard was uneven footing. Grazed bare of vegetation, it was wide enough that none of them had to look over the edge unless they wanted to.

Sam chose to keep her eyes fixed on the space between Ace's ears as he plodded up the trail. When they reached the top, she saw a hawk riding wind currents.

Great, there's something higher up than I am, she thought.

Two things, she corrected her cowardly brain—a hawk and the sky.

"It's like a little plateau," Inez said as the horses tested the rubber mat she'd just explained to Jake. "Ten feet across, at least."

"I don't know about that," Sam said. "The swimming pool in my old school was ten feet deep."

"But it didn't have three horses to fill it up," Inez pointed out.

"And depth and width are kinda different," Jake said. He sounded as if he were talking to a kindergartner.

The only thing that kept Sam from sticking her tongue out at him was the risk of looking like one.

The waterfall whispered as it fell down a gap in the rock. Sam was wondering where the water came from, thinking it looked as if it just welled out of the rock itself, when Bayfire lowered his head to sniff the rubber padding under his hooves, then blew through his lips.

"He's quietin' down," Jake said.

Inez nodded. "He recognizes the smell, I'd guess. Most of his movies use these mats."

Inez let her reins droop and Bayfire moved forward, away from Witch and Ace, to the edge. His ears flicked alertly, listening.

"This is it?" Inez asked, looking back at Jake. "This jump's nothing. Sam, come look at it."

I'm not taking the leap and neither is Ace, Sam thought, but she rode forward just the same.

The cleft in the rock was maybe three and a half feet across. Though the water looked white as it found its way down, it was quiet. The jump would be a little wider than the clumps of sagebrush they'd jumped that morning, but narrower than the gully.

Inez backed Bayfire away from the edge and he moved with collected smoothness.

Sam admired the horse, but she was still thinking of their bunny hopping this morning.

"It won't be more than a hop for—" Sam didn't have time to finish her sentence before surprise snatched her breath away.

Inez sent Bayfire forward, and Ace tried to follow.

"Oh no," Sam whispered. "No more follow the leader."

Ace shook his head, but Sam kept the reins snug. Bayfire moved with the grace of a show jumper and the rubber mats made him soundless. He landed on the other side as lightly as a bird.

Sam still hadn't caught her breath when Inez wheeled the horse back around. And then he was coming at her, taking the jump as easily as if he were stepping over the threshold of the barn.

Sam glanced at Jake and he was smiling, but she wanted to shout or at least applaud. Instead, she hissed, "That's great!" as Inez stopped the horse.

"How fiery did he look?" Inez asked, and Sam didn't know what to say.

Bayfire had lost the flare of spirit. His moves had looked effortless, though, and she thought that should be enough.

"He's poutin' again," Jake said, shaking his head.

"I'm calling it a day," Inez said.

They all did, riding back in near silence.

Clouds had moved in to turn the blue-and-gold morning dark, but it wasn't cooler. If anything, it felt hotter, as if the warm air had been pushed down, closer to them, by the gray thunderheads.

Jake split off, riding toward home with a promise to be back before daybreak. Sam hoped the shoot went off on schedule, though, because Jake had told her he and his mom had to be at the Reno airport by evening.

The neigh Bayfire sent after Witch was melancholy, but Sam took it as a good sign. The stallion was definitely getting socialized. Now, she just had to think of a way to cheer up Inez.

Lunch, Sam thought. She couldn't help smiling when she realized she'd accidentally picked up Gram's solution for sagging emotions.

Hurry, Sam told herself as River Bend Ranch came into sight.

What should she fix? She wasn't a great cook, and her best lunchtime creation—grilled-cheese sandwiches and tomato soup—really wasn't suitable for late August.

A far-off rumble of thunder teased her, but it was still too hot for soup.

Wait. There'd been barbecued steak left from last night's dinner, and there'd definitely be fresh bread and maybe some tiny, sweet carrots from Gram's garden.

They were nearly at the bridge over the La Charla River when Inez blurted, "I don't know what to hope for, Sam."

Inez shook her head as if she couldn't believe what she'd said.

"Sorry, I sound like I'm about ten years old. I don't mean to be dumping my bad mood on you. It's just that if that wild stallion's back up there in the morning, Bayfire will look great." She bent forward and gave the stallion's neck a loud pat. "And he did look fantastic, didn't he? Like a wild beast," she joked with the horse, rumpling his mane. "But his rough attitude could make even that simple jump dangerous."

Sam shook her head. "I'm pretty sure the Phantom won't be back up there again in the morning," she said, but when Inez's faint smile faded, she added, "But he's unpredictable. Since your crew's been in Lost Canyon, setting things up, I wouldn't have expected to see him there today."

"Well, I'm giving my wild beast the afternoon off, so I can drive into Alkali and meet with the crew. He won't need any costuming, which is a good thing since all his plastic armor's in Hollywood, but I'd like to see what I'll be wearing, how early they want me in Makeup and all that."

"Do you have time for lunch first?" Sam asked. "I was going to make us steak sandwiches."

"Thanks," Inez said as she swung down from Bayfire's saddle in the quiet ranch yard, "but I think I'll just clean him up and get on my way."

Inez had brushed Bayfire, cleaned his feet, and put him back in the box stall, but Sam was still squatting next to Ace, feeling his legs for any unusual warmth or sprains from the jumps, when she felt a raindrop plop on her back.

Then, just when she thought Inez had returned to her camper, the woman's shadow fell over her.

When she looked up, Inez was backlit by the sun. Blown by hot wind, the clouds parted for just long enough that Sam couldn't really see her face. Still, something in the way the trainer stood told Sam that something was really wrong.

"There's one little thing I left out when I was telling you and everybody about the family business," Inez said.

"Okay," Sam said. She looked back at Ace's legs, though she was pretty much done. As usual, the tough little mustang had come through the surprise workout just fine. But she thought Inez might be more comfortable if she wasn't standing up, staring her in the eyes.

"When I said my dad was semiretired," Inez went on, "well, he didn't just retire from the equine end of our business. He sold off all our movie animals, except a few he gave to sanctuaries. Then he moved to Miami to live near my brother Mateo. He has a restaurant and my dad's working there a couple nights a week as the maitre d'." Inez swallowed so loudly, Sam heard her. "So, I wasn't exactly lying when I said . . .Yeah I was, but here's the thing. I'm running what's left of Animal Artists, all by myself. So if Bayfire . . ."

Sam stood slowly. Fat drops of rain plopped down on the dusty ranch yard as she tried to figure out what to do.

She didn't know Inez well enough to hug her.

She couldn't promise Inez that Animal Artists wouldn't fail, either, because what did she know about Hollywood? But she did know horses.

"Bayfire's well rested, he's had lots of interesting exercise, time with other horses, and he hasn't made a move to hurt you for a while," Sam said, realizing she'd adopted Brynna's no-nonsense approach to the problem. "You knew what your horse needed and you've given it to him. Bayfire will do great tomorrow," Sam said. "Jake thinks so, too, remember? He said Bayfire looked cured. Not just better, but cured."

"I hope you're right," Inez said dubiously, but Sam saw a little bounce in the trainer's step as she walked toward her camper, jingling her keys, and it hadn't been there before.

Lunch without Inez wouldn't be so bad, Sam was thinking as she turned Ace into the ten-acre pasture. She'd have the kitchen to herself, and eating alone might be fun.

Alone. On some level she must have noticed that Gram's Buick was missing. Now she saw that the horse trailer was gone, too. Then Sam's eyes swept across the pasture.

The rain fell steadily now, and she had to squint at the saddle horses. Dad and the hands had taken the truck, but a horse was missing. Sweetheart.

Sam leaned forward, arms wrapped around her middle as if she were sick. She was, but not with flu or anything like that. Raindrops hammered against the back of her head, drenching her hair until it dripped, too.

The pinto mare was gone, probably forever.

When she ran to the ranch house and threw open the door to demand an explanation, the house was dark and empty.

Only the swing of the grandfather clock's pendulum accompanied Sam as she walked from room to room.

You agreed to this, she told herself, but it didn't help.

With each step, her face felt more sunburned, her hair more dusty, her heart more lonely. She couldn't even find Cougar.

For the first time in months, Sam had nothing to do and no one to do it with.

She was about to start feeling really sorry for herself when she thought of Inez. The trainer was heartsore over her horse, her father had moved away, and she might lose the business she loved.

"Shake it off," Sam told herself, and then Cougar skidded out from under the couch and attacked the toe of her boot. "I'll shake *you* off," she threatened gently, but the cat wasn't scared.

His back arched. His fur stood on end. He pounced on a magazine someone had dropped next to a chair, then raced up the stairs as if Blaze were chasing him. But whatever Cougar was afraid of, was all in his imagination.

Chapter Fifteen ❧

A cool breeze blew through the kitchen window. Sam smelled dry grass crackling under the rain.

She stood at the kitchen counter making grilled cheese sandwiches after all, thinking that there was a certain freedom to being home alone.

When the kitchen door opened, she thought for a second that it might have been snatched wide open by the wind, but it was Dad.

How could she have forgotten that he and the hands were haying? What kind of ranch kid forgot rain could damage hay, ruining an entire crop?

But Dad was grinning as the door slammed behind him.

"Got every bit of hay in before it even started

drizzling," he boasted, "so you'd better make more of whatever it is your gonna throw in that frying pan."

Sam pumped her fist toward the ceiling.

"That's great!" she said, then turned back to the sandwiches she was assembling. The pressure was on to make them especially good, but she smiled as she worked.

When the bread was toasted golden and the cheese was melted and gooey the way she liked it, Sam lifted the sandwiches up with a spatula and thumped them down on plates.

Dad looked more than happy with the result.

"Oh, yeah." His voice was a ravenous rumble as he grabbed the sandwich and took a bite.

"I could cut that," Sam offered, but Dad shook his head.

They both still stood at the counter, eating and drinking glasses of milk, when Dad asked, "How're you doing? I thought you might be a little blue over Sweetheart."

"I'm okay now," Sam said, sighing. "Is that why you came back early?"

"Not really," Dad said. "I was good and sick of haying."

"I know you hate it," Sam said, taking a sip of milk.

"It's not all that bad," Dad said. "Haying's like anything else. You've just gotta look at it with the proper attitude. We've got plenty for ourselves and I'm getting a premium price for what's left from that scallywag Caleb Sawyer. Seems like he's got lots of dudes making reservations for that backcountry hunting operation of his."

Sam shook her head.

"I know," Dad agreed. "That's bound to cause someone trouble, but for now, it's helpin' us out. Caleb has to use hay that's certified free of noxious weeds — like ours — and haul it along with him to feed his saddle horses and pack animals. Maybe that'll slow him and his customers down enough so they don't stir up too much mischief."

Sam smiled. She rarely heard Dad this talkative and she was really enjoying it.

"So you're all done?" Sam asked.

"Yeah, strange thing today, though, I was thinking about this medieval movie Inez and them are shootin', and thinking about what I learned in school, that during the days of the Roman legions, Julius Caesar and his sort noticed that birds followed their troop movements. All kinds of birds, but mostly scavengers," Dad said, giving her a sideways look.

Sam recoiled and shivered a little. "Because the birds learned there'd be —"

"Yeah," Dad said, "stuff left on the battlefields after the day was done.

"Well today, when we got close to the field where

we were finishing up haying, I noticed every telephone wire, power line, fence post and tree was covered with birds, watching and waiting."

"Scavenger birds?" Sam asked.

"Them, and hawks, sparrows, magpies, ravens, every kinda bird you see around here. Once we'd moved through with the tractor, the small birds went after the bugs that fell out of the hay. The ravens went after the field mice from nests we'd turned over and the hawks came down after the gophers from tunnels we'd plowed up."

"That's sad," Sam said.

Dad nodded, but the thoughtful look on his face wasn't melancholy.

"We humans have never been too shy about takin' what we need. This time, at least we left behind a feast for the birds."

Sam tried to agree, but when she put herself in the place of the furry creatures suddenly left homeless and out in the open, she shivered.

"I know," Dad said, again, "here's animals who've been protected all season, just exposed like that—"

For no good reason, Sam pictured Jake, range born and bred, leaving rural Nevada for a far-off college.

"And what do you think happened next?"

"I don't know," Sam said quickly, "what?"

"One of those little critters, some kind of rodent—I'm not sure what, it happened so fast—got up on her hind legs, chattered at a raven, and actually bit him on the claw, right there!" Dad rubbed his index finger as he laughed. "Then the raven flew off and she went about finding her hole in the ground."

"That's amazing," Sam said, and her thoughts circled back to Jake again, thinking of how he'd said stubbornness and determination could take you the same place bravery did.

Sam smiled. Some little rodent had proved him right.

Rain had softened into a fine mist by five o'clock in the morning, when Sam stepped off the front porch. She wore boots, jeans, and a brown hooded sweatshirt over her tee-shirt.

"You should wear a slicker. That's not going to do much but soak up rain, you know," Gram called after her.

"I think it'll stop soon," Sam said. "Besides, we're riding in the truck."

Gram tsked her tongue, but she didn't insist. Sam guessed that since she'd actually eaten her bowl of oatmeal, Gram chose to be satisfied with that.

Bayfire had already been loaded into the trailer, but Inez was pacing beside it and hadn't bolted the tailgate into place yet.

"Do you mind if we take Ace along?" Inez said.

Sam shot Inez a suspicious look and the trainer

held both hands up, laughing. "I've got nothing planned for him except keeping my boy company. Really, Sam, I've been thinking about it, and apparently wild horses are like flint and steel for him."

Sam had no idea what she was talking about.

"No wait, I'll explain. You know how you can start a fire with—"

"Flint and steel," Sam finished, nodding.

She'd actually done that in a science class and remembered the spark that set off a little pile of dryer lint they'd used for tinder. It had made a quick blaze of light. She thought of Bayfire's reaction to the Phantom yesterday. Maybe what Inez was saying made sense.

"Ace is the closest thing we have to a wild horse," Inez added.

"That's fine, then," Sam said, and hurried to catch Ace.

At least he was getting credit from Inez, she thought, remembering how Pepper had implied that Ace was just a dull little horse, and also how much he admired Violette. She wished Pepper was around so she could tell him that Ace was acting as an inspiration to a movie horse.

She was on her way to the tack room for a saddle and bridle when she noticed Inez shifted impatiently from foot to foot. Ace was only along for the ride, Sam thought, so she settled for the halter he was already wearing, and got ready to go.

A halo of brightness rose through the fog above Lost Canyon.

Sam leaned against the shoulder strap of her seat belt, staring through the windshield wipers that were losing the battle to swipe away the fog.

It took Sam a minute to realize the blazing movie lights were making the remote place bright as day, long before the sun rose.

Inez parked the truck. Sam climbed out and breathed in moisture. She smelled wet rocks, the moist herbal scent of sagebrush, and something cooking up ahead.

Like a gray tent, the fog muffled all sounds except for the ones within reach. As Sam and Inez backed the horses and led them toward the movie set, both animals danced on clattering hooves.

Sam's head swiveled from side to side. Her eyes strained, trying to see through the fog, searching for the Phantom. There were no mustangs in sight, but would she see the silver stallion, hiding in the frosty mist?

"I think they're just excited," Sam said to Inez.

The trainer nodded, and Sam really felt their age difference. Inez wasn't worried. She'd worked in dozens of movies, and today was just part of her job.

"Why do they call it Lost Canyon?" Inez asked.

"You're just trying to keep me from being nervous," Sam accused.

"Fat chance," Inez joked. "Really, I want to know, if you can tell me."

So Sam gave Inez the short version of the legend.

She'd just finished the sad story of blue-uniformed cavalrymen slaughtering Indian ponies to put warriors afoot, when the mourning cry of a lone coyote drifted through the fog.

The horses hesitated. Sam shivered and tried to think of something comforting to say. Inez might be the movie expert, but the range was Sam's territory, so she gave a halfhearted laugh and said, "He's out late."

"I'm not scared," Inez said, quickening her pace. "This old canyon will just have to wait for another day to add some tragedy to its legend," Inez said, "because everything's going to go just fine, today."

Sam looked up.

I'm not going up there.

It wasn't just the height that scared her or the fact that Ace wore only a halter. Ace's hooves, hardened from years of galloping over ancient lava beds, were sure-footed. He'd get her up there, but she couldn't shake memories of the cougar that had attacked her in Lost Canyon, and Flick, the horse rustler who'd threatened Jake with a rifle. She would let Inez feel confident and safe as she rode up to the waterfall, but she'd also let her ride alone.

And then, the warmth and brightness of the lights, the scurry of active workers, and the smell of donuts made Sam feel safe, too.

"Does everyone wear headphones?" Sam asked as they tied the horses in a shelter then walked to the area where Inez would be made up.

"Just about," she said. "Keeps things running smooth. I've got to go check on a few things, so make yourself at home, just"—Inez glanced toward a woman whose copper-colored hair curved in a cap around her face—"stay clear of Candice."

Sam noticed everyone was doing just that. Although the movie set was crowded, a space of several yards surrounded the small woman.

Sam wandered around, then noticed someone had led Bayfire into a tent. There, someone actually put some kind of horse makeup on Bayfire and adjusted a lightweight saddle on his back. She felt out of place amid the cameras and cords and high-intensity lights. People with clipboards and equipment rushed around her and there seemed to be nowhere Sam could stand without being in the way.

Dr. Scott, with his blond hair glinting and the lenses of his black-rimmed glasses shining, was a welcome sight.

Sam didn't interrupt his examination of Bayfire.

"Settle down, there," the vet coaxed, and the stallion seemed to understand. "Just settle, boy. I'll be done with you in a minute."

Dr. Scott listened to the stallion's heartbeat, then removed the earpieces of his stethoscope and left the instrument hanging around his neck. "Heart's going a mile a minute," he said to himself. But then, he must have noticed Sam standing nearby, because he turned.

"Hi, Dr. Scott," Sam said, shivering inside her wet sweatshirt.

"Hey Sam," Dr. Scott said. "Big fun, huh?"

"For me," she said. "I don't have to do anything but watch. Is Bayfire okay?"

"Nothing to frown about," Dr. Scott said, patting the horse. "He's just a pretty high-strung animal."

He was, and that probably explained his fast heartbeat, but should she tell Dr. Scott about the mustangs?

"We're ready," Inez announced.

As the trainer took Bayfire's reins from Dr. Scott, Sam noticed Inez wore makeup and a costume that looked a lot like a monk's habit.

"What's going on with your outfit?" Sam asked, but Inez waved her hands.

"You have to see the movie," she said. "If I stand here and explain, we'll lose this 'mystical, magical light' and drizzle they're raving about."

"You're really ready?" Sam asked, pulling up her hood and tying it underneath her chin. Gram had been right about his sweatshirt. She felt like she was wearing a sponge. Despite all the excitement, part of her wanted to get back in the truck and turn up the heater.

Sam glanced at the shelter where she'd tied Ace. He was staying drier than she was.

"Pretty glamorous work, isn't it?" Inez joked through chattering teeth, at the same time that she rubbed Bayfire's neck and watched his face, as if trying to read his mind.

"At least you've only got one scene," Sam said, though she felt a little sheepish. She'd never thought about the discomfort of shooting movies.

Suddenly, Bayfire was rearing.

Inez stepped closer to the horse, so near that Sam's old fear of hooves hitting her head made her duck.

That's stupid, she told herself. She was yards away and Inez knew what she was doing. So did everyone else, Sam noticed, because crew members were scanning the area, looking for someone to blame.

Bayfire came back to earth with a slam of hooves, but he was still snorting and rolling his eyes.

"Easy," Dr. Scott said, and he was moving to help Inez when a quick shake of her head warned him back.

Bayfire shuddered. For an instant, Sam thought the stallion was cold, but then his challenging neigh ripped through the chatter and banging of equipment and she knew the Phantom was back.

"Where?" Inez muttered without turning away from her horse.

But the drizzle formed a hissing gray curtain around them, making it impossible to see.

Sam swallowed. The Phantom could be on any ridge or outcropping, near or far, and Bayfire would probably smell him.

Inez held the stallion's reins, trying to coax him to follow her without jerking on his tender mouth. Bayfire lunged as if he were trying to break Inez's grip, but she managed to hold on.

"Never seen him pull this before," said a short man with shaggy brown hair who was standing nearby.

"He'll be fine, Ben," Inez said, but she shot a worried glance past him. "Just cover for me with Candice."

"Much as I can," he said, following her glance to where the copper-haired woman was obviously correcting someone by shaking her index finger.

Who was she? Sam wondered. Someone important?

"Really, Ben, he'll be fine once I get him up there. You'll get some heart-stopping shots," Inez said, lifting her chin to the cleft at the top of the rock face. "He was spectacular up there yesterday and you know that if she isn't pleased with what she sees, she'll put the word out that he's finished as a stunt horse."

Heart-stopping shots, Sam thought. So, was Ben a cameraman? If so, how could he cover for her with Candice? And if Candice declared Bayfire finished as a stunt horse, did she really have enough influence to hurt him and Inez?

Her job's at risk, Sam reminded herself, and despite the chill, she felt her cheeks heat in embarrassment. Her worries were no excuse for not going up the steep trail with Inez and Bayfire.

But how would they get him up there?

The stallion lunged against the reins as Inez tried to maneuver him into a position where she could mount.

"I don't want to tell you your business," Dr. Scott said, "but if he's friendly with Ace, you might take the two of them up there."

"Is this a setup?" Sam asked the vet. She meant for it to sound like a joke, but apparently her uneasiness came though.

"Why, no it's not." Dr. Scott's eyes considered her as if she were a stranger.

"Sorry," Sam apologized. "I'm not too crazy about heights."

"We'll be fine," Inez said. She swung into Bayfire's saddle with the certainty of someone used to being solitary and strong.

She's giving me a way out, Sam thought. The two of them would do fine alone.

Inez leaned close to the stallion's neck, murmuring, but when she lifted her hand to stroke Bayfire's neck, her fingers were splayed wide, as if Inez were trying to stop them from trembling. It wasn't working.

"We're coming," Sam said, and then, with no more than Ace's halter and lead rope, she took the knee-up that the vet offered, and mounted.

Inez's breath came out in a loud sigh.

"Thanks," she said.

Sam felt good about her decision. It was the right thing to do, but that didn't mean she wasn't nervous.

As they rode up the wet and winding path, she talked to Ace in a whisper so low, only he could hear. "I don't know about this."

Chapter Sixteen ❧

"How're you doing?" Sam asked Inez when they paused halfway up the trail.

She could barely see through the drizzle, but she tried to sound hearty and convinced that everything was going just fine.

"Great," Inez said. "The only thing I like better than the wet-dog aroma of this costume is the way it feels like sandpaper against my neck. Oh, and the fact that nothing makes Candice happier—she's the assistant producer and holds the moneybags, if you get my meaning—than when other people mess up and she can gossip about it. It's like she makes herself bigger by making others smaller." Inez took a deep breath. "But we're not going to mess up, are we, boy?" she said to Bayfire.

A few minutes later, Inez shook her head as if she'd just realized Sam was still there, and asked, "How're *you* doing?"

"Okay," Sam said, and she meant it.

She rocked back, balancing on her seat bones like she had when she'd first learned to ride. She exhaled and, despite the bony ridge of Ace's spine, Sam relaxed.

"Move with the horse," Jake had told her all those years ago. "Then you'll never be surprised."

Smiling, Sam even felt brave enough to peer off the trail's edge, to all the lights and cameras down below. On the edge of the swarm of activity, she saw a truck that looked familiar.

"Hey, I think I can see Jake and his mom and—" Sam straightened, tightening her legs around Ace just to stay upright. "Whoa, boy."

Then, she turned toward Inez, who was holding a hand out as if checking the quality of the rain, and asked, "Why would Pepper be here?"

"I don't know," Inez answered, gathering her reins and urging Bayfire forward once more. "Who's Pepper? If he's not some guy who's going to save my neck if we miss this drizzle—"

"Never mind. I'm just being paranoid," Sam said, but she wished she hadn't seen Pepper. "It was definitely him."

The only thing that would get him up here on a day

off after haying was Violette Lee. Sam just knew it.

Okay, that's not so weird, Sam thought, trying to ignore the drumming of her heart. *As long as she's down there and not up here, what's the problem?*

Still, the possibility that Violette was down below made Sam glad to reach the top of the cleft rock.

"Ben's giving me the go-ahead. Let's get this done," Inez muttered, looking down toward the cameras.

As if he understood, Bayfire shied away from the edge. He tossed his head and backed, though Inez's legs clamped so hard against him, Sam could see the trainer urging her horse forward.

"He's not going to jump," Inez said.

"He can smell the Phantom," Sam said gloomily.

"So, he's got the fire he's been missing, but he's got more attitude than—" Inez groaned in frustration as the stallion planted his feet, flattened his ears, and snorted.

"Candice is watching, boy. Just give me one jump," Inez begged the horse, but then she turned toward Sam.

Even in the drizzly darkness, Sam knew what the trainer was thinking. Yesterday, the horses had played follow-the-leader and neither had failed to imitate the other. They were herd animals. That's what they *did*.

It didn't matter if the light was dim and the rubber pads a little squishy; Inez wanted her to jump first.

When she closed her eyes, trying to avoid Inez's pleading gaze, Sam saw the image of a furry little rodent biting a raven.

Thanks, Dad, Sam thought with sour gratitude.

Sam stared at the gap in the rock. Ace could do it. No question.

"Piece of cake," Sam said, though the words sounded squeaky. "We'll go first and Bayfire will follow."

"You're the best," Inez said. "I know you don't want to and we could probably—"

"Hold onto your, uh, hood," Sam said.

Teeth chattering with cold and nerves, Sam wheeled Ace into position.

She tried to settle back as she had riding up the trail.

Feel the horse. Don't be surprised.

But her attention veered to the sound of someone down below shouting.

"They think you're me, but they'll keep rolling until Bayfire follows," Inez explained. "Just do it! Sam, go! Now!"

Ace understood. Before she'd touched her heels to him, her mustang gathered himself, lunged forward for a few steps, and then they were flying.

Sam only knew she'd closed her eyes because she opened them in midair. When she did, she saw the Phantom.

That second of distraction cost Sam her balance.

Ace's hooves landed safely on the other side, but he pulled up short, swinging his head left to see whatever Sam had spotted. She slipped to the right, and no matter how she clung to the lead rope and tried to tighten her legs, her weight had shifted too far. She fell over his sleek right shoulder, then hit the rubber mat rolling.

Her grip on the lead rope kept her from going far, but when she stopped, she could see over the edge. If she'd stuck out a hand, she could reach thin air, but she wasn't about to do that.

Any other horse would have bolted.

"You are such a good horse," Sam told Ace, but when she pushed up from the ground, she realized Ace wasn't just being her pal—he was staring at the Phantom.

Over the cliff and down below, the silver stallion stood on a sandstone ledge. Soft rain mixed with mist, making it hard to tell his contours from the pale rock behind him. His mane drifted in waves, but the sudden upward jerk of his muzzle and quick flash of his teeth were primitive, not dreamy.

Dizzy from the fall and the hypnotic sound of the small waterfall, at first she didn't think of Inez overhearing.

"Zanzibar," Sam whispered, but no one could have heard because suddenly the stallions were screaming.

Across the gap, Bayfire's head bobbed, eyes

glinting past a black forelock so wet, it stayed plastered to his forehead. If the stunt stallion decided to jump, thinking he'd be closer to the Phantom, Sam knew she wouldn't be safe on the ground.

Still shaking, Sam climbed to her feet.

"No wonder Bayfire was going nuts," she muttered to Ace as she edged closer to him.

The Phantom was across the canyon, but he wasn't far away. His scent must be everywhere.

"He still won't jump," Inez yelled across at Sam. "Can you come back and hold him for me? I've got another idea, but I've got to go back and talk with Ben."

Jump *back*? Of course she had to, Sam thought.

She couldn't stay here. Could she?

"Maybe just 'til the sun comes out," she told Ace. "It's August, after all. The rain's already slacking off. The sun has to come out sometime."

Sam placed her hands on Ace's side. No one stood ready to give her a knee up. She had to do this on her own. But why did her hands look so pale?

Fish belly white, she thought as she scrambled onto his back. She'd barely centered herself whenAce kicked in high spirits and her weight shifted forward.

"Yeah, you think it's fun," she accused.

Gripping his mane and the single rope rein with both hands, she started backing him for what would be an awfully short running start.

He took two, three—and a half—steps back before he pressed against the bit and took her—

unwilling and unsettled—with him, jumping more perfectly the second time than he had the first.

Sam glanced across the canyon, something moved, but she wasn't sure—was the Phantom still there? She didn't have time to be sure, because Inez was sliding off Bayfire and tossing her the reins.

"What are you—?" Sam broke off. The horses snorted, the waterfall seemed to shush them, and Inez was running much too fast down the path, saying something, shouting, but what?

"Careful of the wet rocks!" Sam yelled, but then she felt silly.

Inez was an adult. She probably knew that the rocks were slippery, that the wet ground was turning muddy, that she could lose her footing and fall.

Sam turned her attention to the stallion.

"Hey, big boy," Sam crooned to Bayfire, but he slung his head away from her so hard, Sam decided to climb off Ace before the stallion jerked her to the ground.

Her legs trembled, but they held her. She dropped Ace's halter rope. She could trust him to stay ground-tied.

Sam was just thinking there was no better horse in the world when she heard a strange rustling sound.

What could it be? Yesterday she'd noticed the path up was clear of vegetation, so it couldn't be someone or something making its way through thick brush. That's what it sounded like and she could have missed seeing it, but sodden bushes wouldn't rustle, would they?

Then she realized it wasn't brush at all.

Petticoats, Sam thought suddenly.

In that instant, Violette Lee appeared. Dressed in flounced pink skirts and a tight bodice cut low on her shoulders, she looked determined, ready to take charge.

"That's it, Samantha, hand over the reins," Violette demanded. She extended her arm, snapped her fingers, and turned her palm over in readiness. "Give him to a professional."

Sam took a deep breath. She wasn't sure what to say, but then her thoughts pushed the words out slowly.

"I don't think I will," Sam said.

Chapter Seventeen ❧

℘ayfire spooked, shying sideways.

"Silly, silly boy. You didn't let her ride you, did you?" Violette chided the horse, then barked at Sam, "Did he?"

"No," Sam said, but Violette's head tilted to one side and her eyelids were half lowered. She wasn't convinced.

"Even if you did, your scene will be erased." Violette hissed the last word. When Sam took a step back, the actress reached for the reins again. "I can handle him!"

With Ace and the stallion jostling together on the small plateau, Sam wasn't so sure.

She thought of Violette buzzing the cattle in her

plane, and being rude to Gram and Brynna behind their backs. She thought of Violette waltzing past her in her own yard, as if she didn't even exist.

She remembered Jake saying Violette needed to be told she wasn't a princess, but Jake was wrong. Violette knew she was no princess. She just acted that way so people wouldn't know she was still a scared little girl who only felt at home with animals.

But Violette could do a lot of harm while she was pretending. Sam had to stop Violette from hurting the horses, and herself, if she could.

"Get out of here." Sam kept her voice level, knowing nothing but an order would get the actress's attention. "There's no room to fight."

For an instant, Violette looked bewildered. She glanced at the wet and gleaming rocks around her, then gave a cold laugh she could only have mastered for a movie.

"No room to fight," she repeated. "You should be grateful for that, you dirty little cowgirl. Now give me Bayfire." Violette looked up at the stallion, and a question came into her tone as she insisted, "He loves me!"

Sam could read horses, and she knew the stallion didn't love anyone right now. Rearing and staring, Bayfire challenged the dim silhouette across the canyon.

He could see the Phantom as well as smell him, and he'd recognized the other stallion's defiance.

Then Violette saw the Phantom, too.

"What a magnificent mirage of a horse." Her voice was faint, as if the sight of the silver stallion had made her breathless.

Rearing in a dare, Bayfire's shoulder grazed Violette and sent her stumbling. She screamed as she fell.

A gasp ripped from Sam's throat.

Violette was so near the edge, Sam released Bayfire's reins and threw herself toward the actress. Arms flung so fast she felt it in her shoulder joints, fingers stretching, reaching, she tried. Sam's fingernails skittered across the pink taffeta skirt, but her hand closed on nothing.

Sam's mind raced, trying to make sense of the neighs, screams, and the sudden darkness around her.

Blinking, Sam realized it was dark because Ace stood over her, protecting her from the plunging stallion who'd set off downhill.

First, Sam looked for the Phantom. He'd disappeared from the sandstone ledge without a good-bye, but then she wondered, where was Violette?

Sam saw Bayfire rear above Inez at the head of the trail.

Inez touched her cheek and Sam knew Inez wasn't injured. It was a signal between the two and Sam hoped it worked.

On all fours, Sam crawled. She tried to get a better view without getting kicked. Ace wouldn't do it on purpose, but he was a horse, not a pet, and being in the middle of four rock-hard hooves didn't make her feel safe. She'd been kicked in the head before, and no matter what Ace intended, he could hurt her.

"Bay!" It was Inez's voice, though Violette was still someplace nearby, screaming for someone to help her.

"Please," Sam whispered as the stallion, amazingly, lowered to all fours.

The rain had dwindled to a few pattering drops.

Sam heard the thump of her own heart as Bayfire danced in place. He wasn't about to let her mount up and jump him over the waterfall, but it was a kind of obedience and probably the best Inez could expect.

Inez must have thought so, too, because she pointed down the path, and the stallion galloped on without her.

Inez looked up at the shifting clouds, and Sam was about to ask if they'd shoot the scene later, when Violette screamed once more and this time Sam understood her.

"My arm is shattered!"

By the time Sam crept out from under Ace, Inez had already gone to Violette.

The sky was light enough now that Sam could make out Violette on her side, knees drawn up amid her pink skirts, one arm curled around her head as if she couldn't bear the pain in her other, out-flung arm.

Kneeling beside the actress, Inez glanced up, took

in Sam and her horse, and nodded.

"I wondered where you went." Her businesslike tone reminded Sam that Inez had been a school nurse. "Why don't you go on down. I have a feeling it's going to get pretty crowded up here soon, and I'd like to know someone's taking care of my horse."

"Are you sure?" Sam asked. From where she stood, she could see Violette's eyelids were squinted closed and she was biting her lip.

"I'm sure," Inez said. "It's just a sprain."

At that, Violette made a keening sound and Sam moved closer. The actress sounded awfully miserable, Sam thought, but then Violette's eyelids opened and she glared.

"You think you're quite the little wildcat, don't you?" Violette snapped.

Sam looked down at Violette, wanting to tell the actress that it was her own fault if she was hurt, and that it would have been her fault if she'd injured Sam or Ace or the horse she claimed to love.

She wanted to, but she didn't. This was no time for a showdown. Besides, Jake wasn't here to watch.

"Sam," Inez reminded her, "if Bayfire's taken off, find the emergency bucket of grain. That always works."

"Right," Sam said, but then, before she could leave, Inez stopped her.

"Whatever you do, don't talk to Candice until I can see what Ben shot. Okay?"

Bayfire hadn't jumped, so the cameraman couldn't have gotten anything useful for the movie. Could he?

But Inez's voice sounded so pleading, that Sam just said, "Sure." Then she hurried down the path, leading Ace.

A figure was lurching up the path and it only took her a second to recognize Pepper.

"She's fine," Sam called to him.

"Thank goodness," he answered with a worried smile, and he ran right past her.

Ace wanted to hurry, but Sam didn't let him. This was no time to fall on a rain-slickened rock.

When Sam reached level ground, Jake was waiting.

"Didn't mean you had to break her arm," he joked.

"What?" Sam gasped. "Oh, you mean Violette?" Sam let out a breath and a shaky laugh. "Sorry you didn't have a front-row seat, but actually, it wasn't very exciting. She broke her own arm." Then Sam shrugged. "Only sprained it, really."

"I figured," he said. "Still, good job up there, Brat."

Of course Jake didn't explain whether he was talking about keeping the horses safe, or jumping, or not pushing Violette all the way off the edge, but Sam didn't care. She gave him a gigantic hug.

Sam had just an instant to think Jake smelled of horses and denim and rain, a pretty nice combination, before he pushed her away.

"Horse isn't gonna put up with much more of this, and I need to head for home," he said, slapping Bayfire's reins into her hand.

"Okay," Sam said, and as Jake stalked away, she couldn't help laughing.

He might have cut his hair and he might be headed for college, but Jake was still Jake.

Sam had settled Ace and Bayfire in the shelter reserved for them, when she smelled the scent of strong coffee behind her.

"Hi, there." Candice the assistant producer stood just behind her. She offered Sam a white Styrofoam cup filled with coffee.

Should she take it? Inez had said to stay away from the "keeper of the moneybags." Not only that, but Sam could see Ben, the cameraman who seemed to be Inez's friend, standing just behind Candice.

He looked jumpy. If he'd been a horse, she would have spoken to him in soothing tones. But he was a person and this was a situation totally foreign to her.

"How you doing?" Candice asked.

Just over the woman's shoulder, Sam saw Ben making a zipping motion across his lips. But she had to say something, didn't she?

"Okay," Sam answered.

"Good, good," Candice said. "The vet's gone up to take a look at Violette, but she's okay, I take it?"

"I'm not sure," Sam said.

"Inez has some medical skills, so she's probably looking at her." Candice's voice went up, but it wasn't really a question, so Sam just stared at her.

"It's a good thing she got Bayfire pulled together," Candice said.

Sam couldn't figure out whether the woman was just making conversation or grilling her for information. Still, she hadn't asked a question, so Sam just smiled.

Candice's lips opened, then closed. She shook her head.

If she's decided I'm not worth talking to, Sam thought, *why doesn't she go away?*

"So much for that," Candice said, turning away from Sam to face Ben.

So much for what? Sam wondered.

"I don't think we'll be sending anyone back up and that jump wasn't half bad," she said as they walked away.

"But—" Sam began. She'd been about to say Bayfire hadn't jumped. She stopped just in time.

"Yes?" Candice said, wheeling on her as if intuition told her something was wrong. "What is it?"

Inez had said Candice loved to catch other people messing up.

Behind Candice, Ben buried his face in his hands.

Sam took a deep breath. She wasn't sure how to get out of this.

"What was it you were going to say?" Candice asked. "Go right ahead," she encouraged.

Oh well, Candice already thought she was a lost cause.

"Uh, do you think I could have a donut to go with my coffee?" Sam asked.

Candice gave a condescending chuckle.

"Take care of her, Ben," she said, then walked away.

Ben gave Sam a thumbs-up sign and whispered, "Nice save."

"Real nice," Sam said, feeling embarrassed, though there was no reason she should worry about what Candice thought of her. "She thinks I'm dumb as a rock."

"So what? She thinks everyone is," Ben said.

It was almost an hour later by the time Dr. Scott had splinted and wrapped Violette's arm at her insistence, and Pepper—proud of the responsibility—had driven her to the hospital in Darton.

Although Inez was eager to load up the horses and get back to her cozy camper where she could change into dry clothes, when the cameraman Ben motioned to her, she pushed back the wet hood of her costume, tightened her ponytail, and looked suddenly alert.

"What's up?" Inez asked.

"I've got something you're going to want to see,"

Ben told her.

Exhausted as she was, Inez hurried over to watch a monitor.

Sam didn't groan, but she wished Jake hadn't already left with his mother. They would have given her a ride home.

Or she could have ridden with Pepper. Still, he'd been hauling Violette with him, and he wouldn't have made a detour to River Bend before heading to the hospital.

Sam imagined that trip with Violette and decided she'd much rather stand here with the horses, even if it meant getting soggier by the second.

"Wow," Inez said, pulling Sam's attention back.

Excitement and disappointment whirled together in that single word and Sam was moving toward Inez before the trainer motioned her over.

Both Inez and Ben looked over their shoulders, searching, Sam would bet, for Candice, before they rewound the film.

"Watch," Ben said, and Sam did.

Somehow the camera's eye had peered through the curtain of rain, turning it to silver mist and there, silhouetted against the sky, she and Ace jumped over the miniature waterfall.

"He looks amazing! It's so dramatic," Sam sputtered. Her little brown mustang looked absolutely magnificent! And then she realized what this meant. "Is that what Candice—?" Sam whispered, but she couldn't manage to finish the sentence.

"At first even I thought it was Bayfire," Ben said, almost under his breath, "and I was watching your whole circus going on up there."

Sam stared at Inez.

"She thinks it's us," Inez said, touching her chest. "Ben says she's happy with the shot and she hasn't made any more remarks about Bayfire being finished."

But the horse leaping that cliff wasn't Bayfire! It was Ace, and he deserved to get credit for his wonderful performance, didn't he?

Sam's heart pounded and she swallowed against the lump in her throat.

If she let the producer think the glorious leap had been made by Bayfire, Inez and the stunt horse would keep their jobs and, more important, their reputations as experts. If she forced the producer to see that the horse in that shot was Ace . . .

Sam looked toward Bayfire and Ace. Her little brown mustang was lipping the stallion's mane, grooming him as he would a best friend.

Ace didn't care whether or not he got credit, Sam realized. It was her. She wanted to tell Dad and Brynna and Gram and Jake and Jen! She wanted to show Violette that—what?

Sam put her hands on her hips and faced Inez and Ben.

The cameraman's frown told Sam he thought she'd be too starstruck to turn down the glory. Inez looked hopeful.

She knows me better, Sam thought.

"What if we make a deal?" Sam said.

"You want the footage I took of the wild horse across the canyon?" Ben blurted.

Surprise whiplashed through Sam. Of course, a man who depended on his eyes for his artistry would have spotted the Phantom. A video of the Phantom!

"Oh my gosh," she gasped.

"You're not a very good negotiator," Inez said, laughter breaking her tension.

"Oh yes I am," Sam insisted, drawing herself up to her full height. "Of course I want the film of the Phantom, but there's more."

"Spit it out," Inez said, still smiling.

"I won't tell a soul it's Ace, if you come back next week and pick out your own wild horse," Sam whispered.

"But how?" Inez asked.

"There's an adoption day at Willow Springs Wild Horse Center next week," Sam said. "Lots of mustangs need homes."

"And that way, Bayfire will have his inspiration whenever he needs it," Inez finished. "Sam, you're brilliant."

The trainer swallowed audibly, then, looking humble as she put a hand on Sam's shoulder. "And the three of us"—she paused to glance across the movie set to the tent sheltering Bayfire and Ace—"I guess the horses make five — know who really stars in that incredible scene."

Sam nodded, surprised that *just knowing* was good enough for her.

"Okay, so I'll be back and adopt myself a mustang," Inez said, and as excitement charged her voice, the trainer glanced toward the mountaintop with a considering expression.

"Oh no," Sam said, following Inez's eyes. "There's one wild horse you can never have." Sam realized she'd been shaking her head with each word and she made herself stop. Still, she couldn't help adding, "You can't have the Phantom, because he's mine."

From
Phantom Stallion
∽ 20 ∽
BLUE WINGS

*A*n auburn braid stood out against the black horsehair. Biting her lip in concentration, Samantha Forster tied the strands cut from her own ponytail into Tempest's mane.

For once, the filly cooperated, standing statue-still, until Sam gave her a pat.

"All done," Sam said, but Tempest only shoved Sam with her nose.

The little plait twisted with Tempest's movements, shimmering like a primitive good luck charm in the August sun slanting through the barn rafters over-head.

Sam had read that some Indian warriors braided their own hair into the manes of their horses so that their spirits would mingle. So she'd made a tight, tiny plait at her nape. Then she tied it top and bottom with yellow thread and cut it off so close to her scalp that the prick of Gram's sewing scissors made Sam jump.

Stroking Tempest with one hand, stroking the filly, Sam used the other to reach to the back of her own neck to feel where she'd cut the braid off. She really hoped it wouldn't leave a bump or gap under the rest of her hair. After all, school started again next week and she'd rather not look weird.

Tempest's small black hooves shifted in the straw. Before the filly turned more restless, Sam talked to her.

"It's just for fun, baby, and to get you used to being handled in any way I can dream up," Sam told Tempest. "I don't actually believe it will blend our spirits, but I wear a bracelet of your sire's hair." Sam paused as Tempest sniffed the bracelet, almost as if she understood. "And this kind of completes the circle, don't you think?"

Tempest's pink tongue eased out to taste the silver-and-white horsehair bracelet. Then the filly glanced toward the pasture outside the box stall, looking for her mother.

"No, I don't think I'll try this with your mom," Sam said.

She looked past the filly to Dark Sunshine. The buckskin mare groaned and rolled, taking a dust bath like any tame horse. Dark Sunshine was far from tame.

Mustang caution about humans still coursed through the mare, but she'd come a long way in trusting Sam.

Right now, for instance, Sam was looming over Dark Sunshine's filly, double-knotting the yellow thread so that Tempest couldn't shake the braid loose. Dark Sunshine noticed, lurched to her feet, then gave a snort and set to searching for a tender blade of grass.

There. Fingertips tingling from the delicate work, Sam stood back with her hands on her hips to consider the effect. Tied just at the crest of Tempest's mane, before her satiny ears, it looked cute.

Eyes closed, Sam hugged Tempest.

"My Xanadu." Sam's lips barely moved as she whispered the filly's secret name.

Sam felt a fuzzy mane against her cheek and she breathed in the foal's milky-sweet scent.

Then annoyed voices clashed with the barn's quiet.

Sam froze.

"I'll explain it to you one more time." The voice belonged to Sam's stepmother. Brynna spoke slowly, with forced patience. "I've been told to order more wild horses off the range—"

"Fine with me," Dad said. "Makes more room for cattle."

What? Sam's throat tightened. This wasn't the first time Dad had taken sides against the horses, but it still shocked her.

"Which species does more damage to the range?" Brynna asked, but she didn't wait for an answer. "Think of solid hooves like horses have . . ." she said.

Sam rested her chin on Tempest's neck, gazed through the open barn door, and watched as Brynna held up fingers curled in a fist.

"And split hooves, like you see on cattle." She divided her fingers.

"Doesn't matter. Those broomtails don't earn a penny for anyone. Cattle do," Dad insisted.

Broomtails? Sam didn't think she'd ever heard Dad use that word. It wasn't like cursing, but it was worse than rude.

Brynna and Dad sounded angrier than she'd ever heard them, but why?

Dad was a cattle rancher and Brynna worked for the Bureau of Land Management, which set rules for grazing livestock on public lands, so of course they disagreed sometimes.

But one minute, they'd been out in the ranch yard, talking about tomorrow's adoption day at Willow Springs Wild Horse Center. The next minute their voices had grown louder, and now Dad and Brynna had begun talking through their teeth.

"—don't even use the same methods to calculate the number of horses and cattle on the range!" Brynna continued. "They count a cow and calf as one animal—"

"But a horse and foal as two," Dad finished. "You told me."

"You have all the advantages," Brynna said.

"*I* do?" Dad asked. "What happened to *we*?"

Brynna caught her breath at that, but she hadn't finished making her points. She stepped closer to Dad and raised her chin, forcing him to look her in the eye.

"You're usually so fair, Wyatt," Brynna said, freckled face flushed with anger.

Sam waited and watched. Her father and stepmother looked frustrated. They wanted to agree with each other, but couldn't.

Bored with Sam's stillness, Tempest ducked out from under Sam's arm and began nibbling her hand.

"Don't eat my fingers, baby," Sam told her filly, but she didn't pull away. The foal's soft lips comforted her.

When Sam looked up again, Dad and Brynna had moved out of sight.

She edged closer to the barn door and looked out to see Brynna's hands perched on her hips. Dad rubbed the back of his neck.

"Is it worth losin' your job over?" Dad's voice was almost a whisper. When Brynna didn't answer, he went on. "You think I'd abuse this land? Why would I do that?"

"I'm not saying you want to do it, or plan to do it," Brynna said, ignoring Dad's first question to answer the others.

That's probably because Brynna could tell she'd

hurt more than Dad's feelings. She'd questioned his devotion to the ranch.

Brynna shook her head hard enough that she almost lost her balance.

Brynna was just past halfway in her pregnancy, and the extra weight in front made her a bit awkward, but when Dad reached out to steady her, Brynna pulled away.

"Cattle outnumber horses—" she snapped.

"People want beef," Dad interrupted. "I aim to give it to them."

"Consider the impact on the range. All you have to do is watch the difference between horses and cattle at a water hole. Wild horses are prey animals. They run in, take a sip of water, and back off, afraid something might be sneaking up on them—"

"And cattle aren't prey animals?"

"They were once," Brynna conceded, "but it's been bred out of them, and you know it, Wyatt. We've both seen those trampled-out water holes after our herd drinks during a cattle drive."

"You expect those cows to be rangeland biologists like you?"

Sam sucked in a breath. Dad was almost never sarcastic. She was starting to really worry about this fight.

Then, Brynna's face was transformed with a smile.

"What are you thinkin'?" Dad asked, suspiciously.

"It's nothing," Brynna said. "Just something I read in one of our baby books. It said parents are supposed to give their children roots and wings, and I can't help thinking it would be good for parents to have both, too."

"What kind of nonsense is that?" Wyatt asked.

As Brynna's smile spread wider, Sam's spirits lifted. She was related by blood to Dad, but her feelings often matched Brynna's.

No matter what Brynna claimed she was talking about, Sam knew better. When her stepmother looked that happy, it involved a horse.

"You don't remember how smart mustangs are," Brynna said.

"So we're talkin' about horses again?" Dad asked, looking truly confused.

Voice filled with sympathy, Brynna answered, "You haven't ridden one since you owned Smoke."

Goose bumps pricked down Sam's arms. Could Brynna honestly believe Dad would adopt a wild horse?

Tempest breathed in Sam's ear, giving her the shivers, so Sam tried to include the filly in the conversation.

"They're talking about Smoke. He was your grandfather," she told Tempest, but Sam's mind had already strayed to another black foal.

Sam sighed. The Phantom had looked exactly like Tempest when he'd been a baby, when he'd been hers.

"Smoke wasn't smart. He was just darn good at self-preservation," Dad corrected, but Brynna wasn't listening.

Brynna's eyelashes were almost closed as she recited the qualities of wild horses.

"And they've got the best feet in the world. They're well adapted to poor-quality forage, which means they're cheaper to feed. They're levelheaded, too, which is why you have your daughter mounted on one."

Ace, Sam thought. Dad couldn't forget Ace.

Brynna wore a self-satisfied look as if she'd won a debate, and Sam knew that when it came to Ace, her own mustang gelding, everything Brynna had said about wild horses was true. There was no way Dad could deny it.

He didn't, but he was one jump ahead of Sam, because he seemed to have figured out where Brynna's argument was headed.

"Don't go gettin' any crazy ideas," Dad said.

He actually shook his finger at Brynna. Sam braced for Brynna's anger to flare again, but her stepmother just linked her hands behind her back and cocked her head to one side, grinning. Despite the bump of the baby beneath her uniform shirt, Brynna looked girlish and smug.

"With that adoption day coming up, I know you'll have plenty of *loco* leftovers," Dad said, "but you're not bringin' even one of 'em home."

"I'm not?" Brynna asked the question lightly, but Dad heard the dare in her tone and he didn't cross her.

He shrugged.

"I'm going to work," he said, pulling his hat brim lower on his brow as if that ended their discussion. But Dad didn't move away. He scuffed one boot in the dirt and cleared his throat. "About that doctor's appointment of yours —"

"You don't have to come," Brynna said.

"Of course I do, honey."

Sam's worry faded as her father and stepmother kissed.

As their kiss ended Brynna said, "I don't have to choose sides, you know? I can stand here and look clear-eyed at the truth and still love you, this ranch, and wild horses, too."

Dad grumbled, but Brynna just strolled off toward her white truck with the Bureau of Land Management symbol on the door. Her keys jingled as if she were playing joyful music.

"I'm going to go talk with Dad," Sam said, giving Tempest one last hug. "And ask him if he thinks it makes a difference that you're not really broken to lead. You just follow."

Tempest pressed her nose as far out as her neck would reach, and shook her shiny black head.

"Yeah, well, I still think I'll get another opinion," she told the filly.

Tempest sneezed.

Brynna's truck had almost reached the bridge over the La Charla River when she slowed down.

Halfway across the ranch yard, herself, Sam looked around to see if Brynna was avoiding a hen that had darted in front of her.

Dad didn't watch the truck. He squinted at Sam. His eyes narrowed as if he was wondering how much she'd overheard.

But Dad looked away from Sam at the sound of Brynna slamming the truck into reverse. She backed up in a straight line, right toward them, with her arm extended out the driver's side window.

"She's wagglin' her cell phone at me," Dad said in a kind of wonderment. "What's that mean?"

"I don't know," Sam said. Cell phone reception was so spotty out here on the range, Sam almost agreed with Dad that they only seemed to work when you didn't want them to.

"Talk to Jed," Brynna called. "I'm going to be late."

Jed Kenworthy was foreman of the neighboring Gold Dust Ranch and father to Sam's best friend Jennifer. Sam had a single second to wonder why he was calling before Brynna tossed the phone toward Dad.

It was a totally un-Brynnalike thing to do, Sam thought. Her stepmother must have broken off in mid-conversation, too. As the phone sailed toward Dad, Sam was pretty sure she could hear someone talking.

Read all the Phantom Stallion Books!

#1: The Wild One
Pb 0-06-441085-4

#2: Mustang Moon
Pb 0-06-441086-2

#3: Dark Sunshine
Pb 0-06-441087-0

#4: The Renegade
Pb 0-06-441088-9

#5: Free Again
Pb 0-06-441089-7

#6: The Challenger
Pb 0-06-441090-0

#7: Desert Dancer
Pb 0-06-053725-6

#8: Golden Ghost
Pb 0-06-053726-4

#9: Gift Horse
Pb 0-06-056157-2

www.phantomstallion.com

#10: Red Feather Filly
Pb 0-06-056158-0

#11: Untamed
Pb 0-06-056159-9

#12: Rain Dance
Pb 0-06-058313-4

#13: Heartbreak Bronco
Pb 0-06-058314-2

#14: Moonrise
Pb 0-06-058315-0

#15: Kidnapped Colt
Pb 0-06-058316-9

#16: The Wildest Heart
Pb 0-06-058317-7

#17: Mountain Mare
Pb 0-06-075845-7

#18: Firefly
Pb 0-06-075846-5

AVON BOOKS

An Imprint of HarperCollinsPublishers